CHAOS WE UNRAVEL

2

A Watson Twins Mini Mystery

CHAOS WE UNRAVEL

Chelsea Michelle

Chaos We Unravel

© 2023 by Chelsea Michelle (Amanda Tero and A.M. Heath)

Published by Chelsea Michelle
Tennessee

Scripture taken from the New King James Version®. Copyright © 1982 by Thomas Nelson. Used by permission. All rights reserved.

This novella is a work of fiction. The characters in this story are fictitious. Any resemblance to persons living or dead is coincidental.

_____

Cover design by Amanda Tero
Images from
    www.shutterstock.com
Used by permission.

Formatted by Amanda Tero

BOOK LIST

The Chelsea Michelle books are comprised of two series. Mini Mysteries (novellas) and Mysteries (novels).

Here is our recommended reading order.

Hours we Regret (Mini Mystery #1)

Chaos we Unravel (Mini Mystery #2)

Transactions we Expose (Mystery #1)

DEDICATED TO

Our newsletter subscribers of July 2023
We threw this one at you, and you did not disappoint.
You made writing *Chaos we Unravel* so much fun!
Thanks for being with us from the very beginning!

CHAPTER 1

CHELSEA

Where was Michelle?

I shifted the two bagged lawn chairs from my right shoulder to my left and scanned the crowds. She said she would be here at 6:00 sharp. It was 6:02.

I pulled out my phone and swiped to her name.

"Impatient much?" a chipper voice behind me asked.

I spun around. "You're late."

She gave me a mischievous grin and pointed her thumb backward. "His fault."

"Hey now, I wasn't the one putting on the final touches of my makeup." Our older brother, Justin, came out from behind Michelle and wrapped me in a bear hug.

"When did you get in?" I squealed as I hugged him back.

"An hour ago. So don't you dare let Shells tell you I'm the cause for her tardiness."

"Okay, okay…" Michelle gave up with a flick of her wrist.

Justin grabbed the chairs from my arms and added them to the one he already had slung over his shoulder. "Where to?"

Michelle narrowed her eyes to pick the perfect spot to settle down for the evening. "There."

We wove around the clusters of townspeople to a small piece of empty space.

Justin dumped the chairs to the ground.

"Not too close to the pond for mosquitoes, and close enough to the crowds to catch all the action." A broad smile splayed across Michelle's face as she unfolded her chair.

I nestled my chair next to hers.

"Now…" Michelle pointed at me with a dramatic flair. "You're on snow cones. I'm on hamburgers."

I grinned. "One root beer for you, one pina colada for me, and …?" I looked expectantly at Justin.

He threw up his hands. "Really? Root beer all the way."

"Got it." I raised an eyebrow at him. "And what will you do while we get all the goods?"

"Wander." He gave me a broad wink. "I'll probably come back with my own goodies."

I grinned as I grabbed my slim wallet. The snow cone stand was just a few yards away. We were part of the early crowd, but seven people were already waiting. I smiled and nodded as I met the eyes of a few customers from my bank.

"Mama, Mama, Mama!"

The excited voice made me turn. I recognized the little girl grabbing her mom's hand. They came into the bank on occasion. I wracked my mind to place the name of the mom. Brandi. Brandi Callagan.

"I want blue raspberry!" The little girl pointed at the snow cone stand.

"No, *I* want bue ras'erry," Brandi's toddler called from his dad's arms.

The baby in the stroller blew her own raspberries as she caught my eye. They were an adorable family of five.

Brandi glanced around with a tight look on her face before she cheerfully said, "Remember, Mommy said we weren't buying anything today."

"Moooom!" The excitement in the girl's face melted into a thundercloud.

My heart went out to her. With three siblings myself, I had a few experiences of my own where my parents didn't have extra cash on hand for pleasures. Would Brandi be offended if I offered to buy the kids a treat? I didn't remember their exact bank account contents, but I remembered enough to know that things were tight.

At the girl's first wail, Brandi clutched the diaper bag slung over her shoulder and gave her husband a panicked look. He knelt down and said a few words to the girl.

"Holding up the line?"

I jumped at Jenna's voice so close to my ear.

"Sorry." I looked sheepishly at the five feet of space between me and the line then jogged to get back in place. I glanced back at the small family. One of the little girl's hands was in her daddy's and the other held a sucker as they walked away from the snow cone stand. I guess they had their solutions.

I ordered my snow cones and waited while Jenna ordered hers.

"Sit with us?"

"Of course."

"Good. You can carry my extra." I put the third snow cone in her free hand, then bit off the very top of my snow cone. I couldn't wait to use the spoon for that first bite. The cold burst of sweet pineapple and coconut combatted the sweltering heat of the summer evening perfectly.

"You're welcome?" Jenna teased.

"Mhm…" I shivered as the icy cold treat slipped down my throat.

11

As we walked back toward our chairs, low angry voices caught my attention.

"I'm telling you, I know she bribed him."

"You don't know that."

"I do! He as much said that I had it. She couldn't have gotten it on her own merit."

The voices faded off, and I dared a glance behind me. "Do you know who that was?"

Jenna frowned. "Clarice Jasper and… I'm not sure who else. I guess Clarice isn't getting the citizens' award tonight."

"Was she nominated?"

"Yep. Her and Alexis Jones were the two most promising. I heard Clarice was getting it, too. Not that you can always trust town gossip."

"You usually can't trust gossip."

I settled into my chair and motioned to Michelle's. "Did you bring a seat?"

Jenna tilted her body so I could see the chair bag hidden behind her oversized bag. "Yep. I thought about a blanket, so I brought that too. Who knows? I might use both."

I grinned as I set the extra root beer snow cone in the cup holder and leaned into the back of my chair. A smile crept onto my face involuntarily as I soaked in the laughter of children and the murmuring waves of adult conversations. It wasn't often that the park's lawns were covered with so many picnic blankets and lawn chairs. This was Maple Springs at its finest.

"Remind me later," Jenna said, "I've got something for you in the car."

"A puzzle?"

"Maybe …"

I grinned. Jenna knew how to choose the best puzzles.

"Hey, Sea. Jenna."

I glanced up at Kyle Miller, decked out in his police uniform. "Hey back."

His eyes scanned the crowd as we spoke. Occupational hazard.

"Try to let yourself have some fun," I quipped.

He grinned at me. "Oh, I heard there's apple pie in the pie contest. I'll have plenty of fun." He winked as he walked away.

One day, I would get over the regret that he'd never be my brother-in-law.

"You know, there's always a chance," Jenna said.

I quirked an eyebrow at her.

She snorted. "I know those longing looks you send Kyle aren't for yourself."

I hid behind a bite of snow cone. "That obvious?"

"To me, yeah."

"Well, I still think Michelle's a fool for letting him go. But I do think her mind's made up about him."

CHAPTER 2

MICHELLE

Charcoal smoke filled the air as I strode closer to the hamburger stand, where Freeda and Mac Anderson were grilling their fresh beef patties. I stepped in line behind a lanky college guy.

"Matching your sister today?" A warm voice chuckled near my shoulder.

"We thought you'd get a kick out of that," I said, flashing a smile at my ex-boyfriend, Kyle.

"Whose idea was it?"

"Both of ours."

We stepped forward.

"I should have guessed," he said, his eyes roving the mingling crowd.

Maple Springs hosted a grand picnic and fireworks show for the Fourth of July every year. And most years, he was working the event instead of enjoying it.

"Were you planning to watch the show with us?"

"I can't promise anything. It'll depend on how the crowd is acting."

"Do you want me to pick up some food for you?"

He smiled down at me. "I might grab something later. I'm saving room for the apple pie."

"If you need someone to stand in line for you, just holler."

"Thanks."

He craned his neck, his eyes narrowing. "I better keep moving."

I looked in the direction he was walking in, but I didn't see anything out of the norm.

The guy in front of me stared at some other college kids. He shifted, gripping his backpack straps with white knuckles.

I eyed the group.

There were five college kids. Three boys and two girls.

One girl was on her phone, two of the guys were talking to each other, but the third guy was grinning at the other girl.

She tightened her ponytail, then playfully swatted his arm.

He leaned in and whispered something.

"Ummm, are the two of you in line for burgers?"

I snapped to attention at the impatient woman's voice behind me.

"Sorry," I muttered.

The boy didn't seem to notice.

I nudged him. "The line's moved."

He blinked back surprise and grumbled an apology before closing in the line.

A minute hadn't passed before his gaze drifted back to the pair.

Poor guy.

Minutes later, I was turning away from the diner's booth with three fully dressed hamburgers.

"H-hi, Michelle!" Stuart stopped in front of me. "Are you having a good day?"

"I am. Are you?"

He nodded. "Yeah, I can't wait for the fireworks."

"Me too. They're my favorite."

Stuart pulled out his cell phone from his pocket.

I knew what he was going to ask before he asked it because we'd done this several times.

"Can I … get a picture with you?"

"Of course." I stepped closer and smiled into the camera.

He snapped it.

"Hang on, let me get mine. Can you hold this?"

He reached for one of the plates and I slipped my phone out and took another picture of us. It was hard to have a favorite customer since we had so many amazing regulars, but Stuart was certainly among those at the top of my list.

The crowd cheered from the baseball field. Stuart and I instinctively turned to the noise.

His eyes lingered on the action in the distance. "Are you having a good day?"

I smiled to myself at his often repeated question. "I am, thank you for asking. Are you having a good day?" After I put my phone away, he handed me the plate.

His brows dipped together. "Is Chelsea here?"

"Yeah." I pointed in the direction of our seats. "So is our older brother."

He relaxed. "That's good. My parents are here too."

I smiled. "That's good."

The baseball crowd cheered again, tempting our attention toward the noise.

Stuart nodded again and stepped away. "I better go see this game."

"Enjoy!"

He started for the field as he called out. "Have a good day!"

I turned to his fleeting back. "You too!" I headed for our chairs.

A twelve-year-old boy darted in front of me.

I gasped and stopped mid-stride.

Three more wove through the crowd right behind him.

The last one clipped my hip and scratched my wrist with something.

"Ouch!"

The burger plates wobbled in my hands, and I teetered forward with them before righting myself. I glared at the boys' backs.

"Are you okay?" A warm hand touched my arm. He sucked in a hiss. "He did get you pretty good."

"What?" I eyed my wrist from around the plate where it stung. Dots of blood rose along the line, not quite enough to mop up, but enough to leave a line of tiny scabs for the night. "What did he scratch me with?"

"The sticks from a bundle of bottle rockets."

I huffed.

"Nice burger save, though."

"Th–" I lifted my gaze and met his warm brown eyes. He had a natural, manly scruff on his face. Not the sort that was manicured to death, but the kind that looked amazing without much effort. "Thanks," I finished with a smile.

His eyes lit up as he grinned back. "You're welcome. I'm Conner Maxwell, by the way."

He looked like a Conner … A really good-looking Conner. "I'm Michelle Watson."

Conner shifted. "Have you, uhh, had the watermelon yet?"

"No."

"You should. It's fantastic this year. I should know … I grew it myself."

"Impressive."

He winked. "Do you want some … on the house?"

"Sure." I walked beside him to the nearby table under the shade of a canopy. A matronly woman, likely his mother based on the matching shades of light brown hair, took money and organized the pre-served triangular slices.

Conner put three slices on two plates and extended them out to me.

Too late, I lifted the burger plates in my hands.

His cheeks tinted. "How about I walk you back, then?"

"Sounds perfect." And, boy, did it!

A shadow fell over us and a throat cleared. "Ditching your date already?"

My mouth fell as I stared back at Justin.

"After begging me to come here with you, this is how you treat me?" Justin wagged his head. "I am both hurt and shocked."

Conner turned as red as my shirt. "Hey, I'm sorry, man." He extended the watermelon plates to Justin. "I should have asked first. Y'all enjoy."

Justin took the plates from him.

Conner wasted no time zooming away from us.

I watched in stunned silence. Glaring at my brother, I said, "Remind me why I take you places."

He laughed and leaned forward to bite the tip of one of the watermelon triangles. "This is amazing."

"Again. *Why* are you here?"

Justin bumped me with his shoulder. "To keep the riff-raff away."

I groaned and stalked beside him back to our chairs.

Male shouts came from the direction of the baseball game. This time, it wasn't the enthusiasm of a crowd.

"What in the world?" I asked.

"I don't know, but we can see better from our seats, come on."

I scurried behind him in time to see the two men shouting in the grass, halfway between the field and the parking lot. One wore a ref's black and white striped shirt. The other wore a green baseball uniform for the local adult league.

"You need glasses if you think Gary was safe!"

"You're just a sore loser!"

"I'm not going to have anyone talk to me like that!"

"Yeah? Then do something about it."

"Sheesh," Justin muttered. "Where's that boyfriend of yours when you need him?"

"Shut up."

I handed the plates to Chelsea but kept my eyes on the men who were now storming into the parking lot.

"Where did they go?" Kyle asked, suddenly standing between me and Chelsea.

"Somewhere on the other side of the white truck," Justin said.

Kyle charged in that direction.

Smoke filled my nose. I whirled around.

Thick smoke swelled out from the base of the podium where the mayor and his secretary talked.

"*Fire!*" Chelsea and I yelled together.

I rushed after Kyle, yelling his name.

He turned to me and slowed down.

I grabbed his arm. "There's a fire!"

"What?" he said, turning in the direction I pointed.

We raced back together. Once we reached my siblings, a gunshot rang out from somewhere in the parking lot.

A woman's blood-curdling scream tore through the air.

Heart hammering in my chest, I was torn between the two disasters.

Face like flint, Kyle spoke into the radio on his shoulder, calling in the fire and gunshot.

Kyle gripped my shoulders, his eyes centered on the direction of the possible gunshot. "Y'all, stay right here." Without another word, he tore off through the crowd and into the direction of the unknown.

I met Chelsea's concerned gaze.

Stay here?

"Yeah, right," I muttered, striding after Kyle.

"Michelle Renee!" Chelsea groaned behind me.

CHAPTER 3

CHELSEA

Michelle was going to get herself killed someday.

"Michelle, wait!"

Either my twin didn't hear me or chose to ignore me. I took a step forward, but Justin grabbed my arm.

"I'll babysit her for you." He gave me a broad wink, then ran after Michelle.

That only made me feel marginally better. Justin and Michelle were always the ones to get into scrapes. Why wasn't our oldest brother, Ryan, here to keep them in line?

Shouts came from the smoke that was completely opposite of the gunshot sound. An officer led the mayor and secretary away from the smoke while he spoke to the people closest to the fire. I couldn't make out the words, but I could tell by his gestures he was telling them to clear the area.

An older man with an American flag shirt rushed to the smoke with his gigantic water jug and doused it.

A woman grabbed her two toddlers and jogged away from the smoke.

A college kid rushed from the scene, then stopped and bent over, hands on knees. His wracking coughs tore at my own chest.

21

He fumbled in his backpack and pulled out an inhaler. Smoke was probably a terrible trigger for asthma.

A middle-aged group–it looked like two married couples– took two steps back, but continued to stare at the scene. If Michelle were here, she'd be with that group.

Two more men joined the American flag guy and added their own water to the fire. The smoke was now just a wispy curl.

"They're going to need some water to drink now," Jenna said.

I glanced at her. "You're right." I eyed her oversized tote. "How many do you have?"

"Eight."

"Well, it's a start."

We divided the water between us.

I hurried over to the college kid with the inhaler. "Here's some water."

He looked at me, his eyes wide with panic. "Th-thanks," he sputtered between coughs. He grabbed the water and continued walking further from the fire before I could ask if there was anything else I could do to help.

I looked toward the fire–which was now just a haze of smoky residue. The three men walked away from it with their empty water jugs in hand, sweat pouring from their foreheads.

Michelle would never forgive me if I didn't at least try to figure out what had caused the fire. I had three bottles of water left. Perfect. I could do this. I could.

Four boys dashed past me, almost running me over. I clutched my bottles and froze until they passed, then sucked in a deep breath to bolster my courage and marched forward as if I had no ulterior motive.

"Would y'all like some water?" I held out the three bottles.

"Thanks ma'am." The oldest man grabbed a bottle and downed half of it before taking a breath.

"Y'all worked quickly to put that out. Thank you."

One of the younger men shook his head. "Smoke bombs."

My heart rate finally slowed down just a fraction. "Not a fire?"

"Nah." The oldest man finished the water and crushed the bottle. "If that's a prank, it's a stupid one. Someone could have been hurt." He nodded toward me. "Thanks for the water, miss."

They walked away, and I could hear Michelle's ominous voice in my mind, *Unless it wasn't a prank.*

Sometimes I wished I didn't know my sister so well. It was bad enough to have her voice of doubt in person—much worse when she wasn't even here and I heard it.

But if it wasn't just a prank ... what else would it be?

I scanned the area. A few people still lingered near the podium where the smoke was. The half dozen chairs reserved for the mayor and other officials were empty. An officer stood just a few feet from the scene, also scanning the area.

"You're nothing but a thief!"

The voice was low, but intense. I discreetly moved my gaze to the direction of the speaker. I recognized the girl I had seen earlier who claimed the mayor was bribed. Clarice Jasper.

"Oh please, Clarice." The second girl settled her sunglasses in her hair like a headband. "We're not in grade school."

"No, we're not, Alexis." Clarice's large purse swung as she stepped closer to the other girl. "What changed in the last twenty-four hours, huh? Slip the mayor some incentive to change his mind?"

Alexis snorted. "As if he was going to choose you."

"*You* don't need it. The award or the money. And you know I do."

Alexis raised her hand as if appeasing a child. "Honey, the decision is already made. You're doing nothing but causing a scene and further proving why you didn't deserve the award."

Clarice gripped her purse as she glared at Alexis. I held my breath, waiting for something to happen. Instead, Clarice muttered, "You'll be sorry," and stormed off.

Alexis rolled her eyes and walked in the opposite direction.

I made my way back to our seats. Jenna wasn't there. I glanced around for her. She was kneeling beside a woman who was leaning back in her lawn chair.

I walked up. The woman's face was a pasty white, her eyes closed as she intentionally breathed slowly.

Jenna met my glance, and I mouthed, "Is she okay?"

Jenna shrugged and nudged the woman. "Here's some water."

The lady opened her eyes and grabbed the bottle, her hand shaking. "Thanks, dear." She tipped the water bottle up to take a small sip.

"What happened?" I asked gently.

The lady gave a broad shudder. "It was … I swear, it was six inches big. I swear it!"

"What was?" Jenna asked.

"A …" she gave another visible shudder, "A spider. I couldn't help it. I screamed."

My mouth fell open.

She moaned. "This is embarrassing."

Jenna smiled up at her. "Don't be. Everyone's been distracted. I bet no one is thinking any more about it."

Except Michelle. She was definitely still wondering about the scream. But I wouldn't tell the woman that.

"Can we get you anything else?" I asked.

She smiled up at me. "No, darling. I'm feeling better."

She looked better. Color had returned to her face, and she no longer looked close to passing out.

"Thanks, again."

Jenna and I gave a wave, then returned to our seats.

"That is some severe arachnophobia," Jenna said.

"Mhm." I kept myself from glancing back at the woman.

"Convenient timing with the fire though, huh?" Jenna squinted toward the podium where the smoke was totally cleared now.

"I don't think she was faking it, if you're hinting at that."

"She'd have to be a pretty good actress for that to be the case," Jenna agreed.

"Seems like all this chaos is just a facade," I muttered.

"Why's that?"

"It wasn't a fire, but a smoke bomb."

"Hmm…" Jenna's mouth turned downward in thought. "But why?"

"Stupid prank?"

"Or … something more?"

I glared at her. "Not you too."

Jenna shrugged. "It's always a possibility."

I shuddered and stared back at the podium. It was. But why?

CHAPTER 4

MICHELLE

I stood at the edge of the onlookers as Kyle questioned the referee.

The ref swiped sweat off his red forehead, but the baseball player was nowhere in sight.

Justin stepped in beside me. "What'd I miss?"

"Nothing so far as I can tell."

"Boy, he sure looks angry."

I nodded and watched the ref emphasize his words with his hands.

Kyle stood rigid as if waiting for anything.

Two other cops combed the parking lot for the missing baseball player, who moments earlier was seen with the ref heading into the parking lot.

The ref did a double-take and pointed at something on the other side of the parked vehicles lining the grass.

The baseball player paced a grassy hill in the distance.

Kyle remained with the ref while the other two cops raced to meet the player.

"Well, I don't see any bullet holes, do you?" Justin asked.

"Nope."

We eyed each other, the silent question hovering between us. *Then what was this all about?*

"Brandi!" a woman screeched right behind my ear.

Instinctively, I turned to the noise.

The woman had her perfectly highlighted hair in the cutest messy bun. She appeared a few years older than me. She was elegantly tanned and had that classy, magazine model look. It was like she stepped out of an advertisement for "casual" wear from a high-end store.

Brandi, on the other hand, wore comfortable flip-flops and a patriotic shirt that didn't look brand new. She stepped out from behind a stroller with her husband and two kids trailing behind her.

The women hugged, and I turned back to watch the anti-climatic crime scene.

"How are you? It's been forever!" the magazine model said in her shrill voice.

"I'm doing great. You?"

"Looks like you've had another baby since I last saw you."

"We did. Olivia was a surprise, but we're blessed."

"That's so sweet. They're adorable. And they look just like you."

"Thank you."

"I am terrible about keeping up with everyone on social media. I'm hardly ever on there."

"Yeah, I understand. The kids keep me pretty busy."

The model-woman gasped. "Speaking of hardly there ... Jake and I just got back from Hawaii. It was di-vine!"

"That's wonderful! I bet it was pretty."

"Mama," a little girly voice piped in. "I'm done with my sucker. Can we get the snow cone now?"

"You know Blake and I are taking the kids to Florida soon."

"Oh?" came the high-pitched, slightly unimpressed reply. "Florida is nice."

"Well," Brandi cleared her throat, "we're visiting *all* the parks."

"Oh, good. Whew. I thought you were going to the beach. I mean, Florida beaches are nice, but I'm spoiled now thanks to Hawaii." She laughed, and Brandi joined her, though hers sounded a little forced. "I mean, visit the theme parks in Florida but save those babies and take them to the better beaches in Hawaii."

"Mooom! Everyone else has a snow cone."

I smiled at the girl, remembering my own dear snow cone.

"Well, I'll let you get back to your family time. It was nice seeing you."

"You too." Brandi stepped back, snagging the little girl's hand. She caught my eye and gave me a tight smile.

I gave her an encouraging smile before turning back to Kyle. The ref and the baseball player were released.

The crowd of onlookers grew bored and thinned out while the officers talked, but not me. The chances of everything happening at once were too coincidental for my liking. Besides, I still had a cop to interview, while the rest of the crowd didn't.

Kyle strode in our direction and veered off when he spotted us.

The sun beat down overhead. I fanned myself with my collar, missing the icy snow cone I left behind. When he was close enough, I asked, "So what's going on?"

He opened his mouth, likely to fuss at me for asking him questions he couldn't answer, but he stopped and snagged my hand instead, angling it to see the scratch. "What happened?"

"A boy ran into me earlier and scratched me with a ... *bottle rocket*."

Together, the three of us hummed our understanding.

"That was probably what we heard," Justin said.

Kyle's face brightened. "Could be. Let me talk to the others." He stepped aside and spoke on his radio, then returned. "Alright, Rob and Adam are looking for evidence, and I need to find those boys to verify that's what we heard."

"So the men are innocent?" Justin asked.

"It appears so. They came into the parking lot, shouting, then separated to cool off. But I'd feel better knowing there wasn't a gun involved at all in this crowd." Kyle centered on me. "So what do these boys look like?"

I grinned and tipped my head to the chairs. "Let's walk, and I'll tell you."

The three of us fell into step. I gave him a brief description, which wasn't much more than four boys with bottle rockets.

Our chairs came into view but Chelsea and Jenna weren't there. Kyle kept walking while I swung by and grabbed my melting snow cone.

The podium was still standing in a haze of smoke.

Justin squinted into the crowd. "I'm going to check on Sea. A big brother's work is never done."

I giggled.

"You good?"

"Yep."

I scurried back to Kyle's side.

"What are you doing?"

"Helping you."

"I don't need your help, Shells."

"Of course you do. You don't know what they look like."

"*You* barely know what they look like. How much help can you possibly be?"

I grinned. "I know someone who saw them."

He stopped and glared at me. "Why didn't you say that earlier?"

"Duh, so you'd still need me. Then I can tag along." I took a runny spoonful of my snow cone. Most of the ice had melted already. "Just think of it as a ride-along. Now, come on."

He started walking again. "I think they call that impeding an investigation."

"Not true! I'm totally 'peding it."

"That's not even a word!"

"So? I'm still doing it."

He chuckled.

"Besides, I'm the one who brought you your next clue." I lifted my scratched arm for emphasis.

"*I* found the next clue."

"Well, I'm the one who suffered to bring it to you."

His eyes softened. "Are you okay?"

I shrugged. "I'll live." I took another slurp of the snow cone and dangled it in front of him. "Drink. You need to stay hydrated."

He didn't take the Styrofoam cup. "Is this your way of being useful?"

"Aw, come on, Kyle. It's a real live mystery. And I *am* a witness."

He took the cup, moved the spoon out of the way, and downed my snow cone. He handed back the cup.

I stared at the shallow drink at the bottom. "You punk."

"It's the price you pay."

"Fine." I drank the last swallow and threw it in a trash can as we passed by.

"Where are we going?"

"The watermelon stand. There's someone working there who saw the whole thing. He's the one who knew what the boy scratched me with, so I bet he got a better look at them than I did."

I strode up to the watermelon table, but Conner was nowhere in sight. I waited behind an elderly couple before stepping up to the woman selling watermelon.

She smiled warmly, very reminiscent of Conner's warmth. "How many slices?"

"I'm sorry, we're just looking for Conner."

She studied me, her gaze lingering on Kyle standing just beyond my shoulder. "He isn't here right now."

"Can you please call him? It's important."

She shifted uncomfortably, then pulled out her phone and dialed his number. He must have answered because she said, "Someone is at the booth looking for you."

"Tell him it's Michelle Watson."

She repeated my name.

He said something that made her wince.

"We won't take up much of his time," Kyle said. "I just have a few questions for him."

"Umm, there's a cop here with her."

"What?" I heard him exclaim beyond the phone pressed to her ear.

She hung up and sent us a tight smile. "He'll be here in a few minutes."

We stepped aside to let the other customers through.

Kyle's eyes never stopped skimming the crowd. He grunted low in his throat and crossed his arms over his chest.

"Stop looking so serious," I hissed at his side.

"I am serious."

I swatted his arm.

He peered down at me, no doubt with a reprimand about swatting a uniformed officer in public, but he didn't say anything.

"Well, you're scary, so stop it."

"Ummm, can I help you?" Conner asked, circling his mother's back.

31

She watched us, ignoring the child in front of her, holding out a limp dollar.

"I have some official questions for you."

I laid my hand on Kyle's elbow. "We only need to know if you remember anything about the boys with the bottle rockets that nearly ran me over."

"We?" Kyle asked, giving me quite the stink eye.

I shrugged. "You brought me along."

"My first mistake."

"It's the price you pay." I turned back to Conner. "It's official questions, but it's nothing to be afraid of. It happened so fast, I didn't get a good look at them, and I thought maybe you did."

"Is this about that noise? The gunshot noise?" his mother asked, striding to us and dropping her voice to a whisper.

"This is my mother, Leigha Maxwell."

Kyle shook her hand, then Conner's, and introduced himself.

"Are they talking about Ethan and his friends?"

Conner nodded.

"I thought so," Leigha said. "I didn't see them bump her, but I saw them running through here like the devil himself was after 'em."

"Ethan is the only one I know," Conner said. "One of them, the one that bumped you, had on a neon green Under Armor shirt. That I remember. But I think that's it."

"Jacob would be another one," Leigha said. "I'm not sure about the other two, but I bet I could track their names down for you."

"That'd be great, thank you. I'll just wait right here," Kyle said.

Leigha stepped aside and called someone.

Conner walked back to the booth and cleared out the four customers waiting there.

Once he finished, I walked up to the corner of his table. "I, uhh …"

He turned to me, an uncertain look in his eyes.

"I thought I should explain about earlier. That was my brother."

He snorted in an unconvincing way. "You're dating your brother?"

"What?" Kyle said at my side.

My face heated.

"I'm *not* her brother."

I covered my eyes with one hand and groaned.

"Yeeaah, okay," Conner said.

When I looked up, he had walked away again. I turned my fury to Kyle.

"What? I am *not* your brother."

"You're right, you're not. I was talking about Justin."

"Oh." His face darkened.

"I was talking to Conner earlier, and Justin interrupted with his whole ditched date routine. Before I could explain, Conner had walked off."

"And then I put my foot in my mouth."

"Yep."

Kyle winced. "I'm really sorry. People still think we're dating, and I can handle that, but I'm not about to put up with anyone thinking we're related."

I snorted. "Yeah, I get it." The idea of being confused as his sister was pretty disgusting.

"Umm," Leigha cleared her throat. "Excuse me."

We turned to her.

"I have the names you're looking for, and I know where they are, so you can interview them. One of the mothers is holding them. You'll find them along the fence of the baseball field, near the swing sets."

"Wonderful, thank you. I appreciate it." Kyle shook her hand.

I waved goodbye and slipped a glance behind the booth, but Conner wasn't in sight.

Kyle called in the tip to an officer who was closer to the field than we were, and we headed back. No doubt he was taking me back to my family because he didn't trust me to go there alone.

Static from Kyle's radio broke out between us. He slowed to a stop.

I hung at his side.

The message was clear: They found evidence of a fresh firecracker on the back edge of the parking lot.

He met my eyes and sighed. "Well, that's that."

"But that's a good thing, right?"

"Yeah, but I could have done without the wild goose chase." He scratched the back of his neck. "About what happened back there … with Conner. I really am sorry. I didn't mean to ruin things for you."

I waved off the apology. "It's alright. I don't need a guy who scares that easily."

We started again for our seats.

"Thanks for letting me tag along."

He cut me a smirk. "Did I really have much of a choice?"

I shrugged. "You could have handcuffed me to a tree."

"I'll have to keep that in mind."

His radio came to life again, this time, letting us know that they had located the boys. Kyle straightened. "That's my cue."

I met Chelsea's expectant gaze the moment we were near enough.

"The gunshot was a firecracker," Kyle announced in his official tone.

I bit back a smile at how easily he switched on and off his cop mode.

"And the fire was a smoke bomb," Justin said.

Kyle nodded. "I know."

Of course he did, and he didn't bother to tell me a thing.

"Do you think it was set off by the same person?" Chelsea asked.

"That remains unclear." He jutted his thumb at me. "Snoopy here can fill you in on what she knows, but I can't linger."

I wiggled my nose at him for his teasing nickname.

"Hey!" A shout exploded from the podium.

I swung my attention there.

The mayor stood up from his crouched position behind the podium and threw a wild look at his secretary. "Where's the money?"

CHAPTER 5

CHELSEA

My heart leapt to my throat as the mayor rushed toward Kyle. "It's gone! There was $500 cash."

I cringed. Cash was always harder to track down than a check or money order. If that was the case in the confines of a bank, how impossible would it be here in the open air with hundreds of people milling around?

I glanced around while Kyle talked with the mayor in a low voice. There weren't security cameras here in the park. And since the actual ceremony hadn't started yet, I doubted anyone had their phone cameras pointed that direction.

Kyle followed the mayor to the podium.

Michelle caught my eye before trailing behind within listening distance. If she wasn't Kyle's ex-girlfriend, he'd probably arrest her for interference. Not that I didn't think she'd be able to argue her way out of it. She had a way of convincing you her choices made sense.

"C'mon …" Justin grabbed my hand and motioned for Jenna with his other.

"Nuh-uh." I tried to jerk my hand away, but he held it firmly. "*Justiiiiin* …"

He dragged me to Michelle. Thirty seconds later, Jenna joined our group. I glared at her. She was supposed to be the sane one to help me out of these situations. Not join in. She shrugged and gave me a half-smile.

"I think the mayor stole it," Michelle whispered, her eyes focused on the man in question.

"Why?" Justin asked.

"He had the means and opportunity. Shush, I'm trying to listen."

I bit my tongue before reminding her that we weren't supposed to be listening. This was police business. Not Watson siblings' business. Besides, I didn't know what she thought she'd be able to hear above the murmuring of the crowd. I couldn't hear anything since Kyle was intentionally keeping his voice low.

Two more officers joined Kyle. They talked for a few minutes and took notes. One officer taped off the podium. Kyle walked toward us, shaking his head at Michelle.

"What?" she asked, pasting on a sweet smile.

"There's nothing to report ... to you."

Her smile turned into a pout. "You know I'd do everything in my power to help you."

Kyle blew out a breath. "Yeah, that's what I'm afraid of."

"Hey," she hissed. "I helped solve the gunshot sound."

He ignored her and looked at me and Justin. "Y'all can go back to your seats. Please."

"Yes, we will," I said purposefully as I grabbed Michelle and Justin. "We were about to go back anyway."

"No we weren't," Michelle argued.

But they followed me back to the chairs.

"I'm telling you, the mayor did it." Michelle paced with her hands crossed in front of her.

"Why?" I asked.

"Who wouldn't want $500? Besides, maybe he didn't even bring the cash here."

"Except that it is the secretary who handles the money." Perks of being a bank teller. I had this kind of information to hand to Michelle.

"Then maybe she did it."

"Mindy Trapper?" Jenna asked. "I've known her since I was a kid. Her conscience is so sensitive that if she finds a $5 bill in the parking lot and can't find its owner, she always brings it to church and places it in the offering plate."

"And I thought Sea was bad," Michelle muttered.

I rolled my eyes at her.

"I still think it's the mayor. Just because Mindy handles the money, doesn't mean he didn't today. Did anyone see who brought the money to the podium?"

"Why did they even put the money in the podium?" Justin asked.

Michelle snapped her fingers. "I bet it was in a lock box, and they felt it was safe enough. The person who nabbed it must have a bag big enough to hide the entire lock box."

"I thought you said the mayor did it." I couldn't cut the sarcasm from my voice.

"Like any good detective, I'm looking at all the options so as not to be blinded by my true feelings. Besides, the mayor would have the key, not to mention the opportunity to take the money before coming to the podium."

"Oh puh-lease." I sank into my chair.

"So, the mayor is our top suspect."

I hid my face in my hands. I knew without looking that Michelle was holding up her finger as #1.

"But, we're gonna be looking for anyone who'd have a bag big enough to hide a lock box."

I let my hands drop to my lap. "So what? Someone steals it then figures out later how to unlock it?"

"Makes sense to me," Michelle said.

"Yep," Justin agreed.

I resisted the urge to glare at them. They were *not* a good team. Or, maybe they were. And that was the problem.

"Ohhhh ..." Michelle's voice absolutely rang with glee.

I sank deeper into my seat.

"The contestants! One of them could have done it. What are their names?" Michelle looked expectantly at Jenna.

"Alexis Jones and Clarice Jasper," Jenna supplied. "Up until today, the rumor was that Clarice was favored to win. Then all of a sudden, it's leaked that Alexis is winning, and Clarice isn't happy about it."

"Alexis could have done it," Michelle said.

"I would have thought Clarice. She was the one who was upset." Jenna voiced the thoughts running through my mind.

Michelle shrugged. "Yeah, well, that would be too obvious. No one would suspect Alexis."

"But why would she steal her own prize money?" Justin asked. "She was going to get it in just a few minutes."

Michelle thought for a second, then a mischievous grin spread across her face. "To get double the money. She steals $500 and then they wrangle up another $500 to give her the award."

My mouth dropped open. "You're devious!"

"Me?" Michelle gave me an innocent grin. "I didn't steal it!"

"But you thought it up!" Something like that would never cross my mind.

"No, I thought about why *she* would. I would never. If I needed five hundred bucks that bad, I'd go beg Justin."

Justin snorted. "And you think I'd give it to you."

Michelle smiled sweetly and said nothing. We both knew he'd give in.

I mentally replayed the run-ins I had with the two contestants. Clarice may have been a bit hostile, but her interaction with Alexis didn't mean she stole anything. Except … I gasped before I could stop myself.

"What?" Michelle looked expectantly at me.

"Nothing." I couldn't get any lower in my chair. Would it be too noticeable to just leave my sister? Maybe go buy another snow cone?

"That was *not* a nothing. You remembered something. What was it?"

I groaned and nodded.

"What?" Michelle's eyes flashed with excitement.

"Clarice. She … had a large purse."

"She did?" Michelle was way too eager.

"Yeah. And … Alexis may have had a tote." Now I felt bad mentioning it. I wasn't totally sure. I shouldn't have said anything.

"*Chelsea!* Two main suspects are seen by the crime, *both* with bags large enough to easily hide something, and you're just now telling us?"

Nope. Definitely shouldn't have said anything about the bags. "Be glad I told you anything," I grumbled.

I remembered something else and winced.

"What?"

"They were bickering after the smoke bomb went off." That was it. The last thing I was feeding my clue-hungry sister.

"Clarice and Alexis?"

I nodded. "But having a large purse doesn't make you suspicious. *Especially* because Clarice was still onto Alexis about how unfair it was for her to win the prize. Why would she do that if she had already stolen the money?"

"To shift blame from herself," Michelle offered. "If Clarice acts like she's upset after the money is missing, then no one's going to think she stole it."

"Michelle Renee!" I threw my hands up and looked at Justin and Jenna, hoping they were seeing the ridiculousness as clearly as me. "You've already been convinced the mayor, Clarice, and Alexis all did it. This is not how you figure things out!"

"Chelsea Rose, yes it is. It's being thorough in the investigation."

"We're not investigating," I groaned.

"We're about to."

I didn't like the way Michelle was looking at me.

"No, Michelle, we are not."

"Yes, Chelsea, we are. You and Jenna. Me and Justin. We're on the mayor. You're gonna find Alexis and Clarice. Oh no... wait..." Michelle got a mischievous gleam in her eye. "Justin needs to investigate Alexis or Clarice. He's cute enough to get them to talk to him."

Justin fanned his face. "Why yes, I am. Thanks for noticing." He gave me a broad wink.

I rolled my eyes. "Oh brother." Flirting was embarrassing enough as it was. Flirting to gain information that was none of our business was a whole other level. With this type of example, Michelle would never listen to reason.

"Yes, that's what I am, your good-looking brother," Justin said with another wink. Those were getting annoying.

"You are *not* serious about this."

"Why not?" Michelle's voice joined Justin's in perfect unison.

Seriously. Where was Ryan when I needed him? I was severely outnumbered with these two. And there was no way I was going to stand with Justin while he flirted to gain information. I was going to lose him in the crowd and let him do his own thing.

"Okay, I'm on the mayor. Jenna, your mom knows everyone, see if she's heard of anything else suspicious–or if we should add to our suspect list. Justin, you take … well, whichever girl you can find first. And then Chelsea, you're on the other."

Michelle palmed her phone and practically waltzed away.

Jenna shrugged at me before walking off.

"What d'ya say, sis." Justin nudged me with a big grin. "Let's find us some girls."

I was going to die.

"Look, all you have to do is point out the chicks."

"Alexis and Clarice," I muttered.

"Yes, those chicks."

I was pretty sure I was blushing. This was going to be awkward. I scanned the crowd as I trailed behind Justin. Today was supposed to be a fun summer outing. I didn't sign up for detective duty, much less assisting my brother in his flirtation mission.

I scanned the crowds. The sooner we found Alexis and Clarice, the sooner we'd check them off our list. Or Michelle's list.

I squinted at a college girl who was fidgeting with her ponytail and talking to a guy.

"Is that one of them?" Justin asked in a stage whisper.

She turned her face for a brief second, then looked back at the guy.

"No …"

Wait a second.

"What is it?"

Drat. He could read me about as well as Michelle.

"Nothing." I shifted so it wouldn't seem like I was staring at the guy. He looked to be about twenty. His face was filled with excitement as his hands clamped onto the straps of his backpack.

"Sea ..."

"Okay, okay. So I may have seen that guy leaving the smoke bomb. He was having an asthma attack. Looks like he's over it now."

"Hmm ..."

The way Justin drew out the one syllable wasn't sounding good.

"Change of plans," Justin said. "I'm pulling rank over Michelle. You follow backpack dude, and I'll find the chicks."

Nope, I didn't like this plan any better than Michelle's. "You don't even know what they look like!" If I kept looking and we didn't happen to find them, I could say we tried.

"Jenna does though, doesn't she?"

I didn't like where this was going. I hesitated.

"That's what I thought. She's talked to her mom by now. I'll team up with her, and she can help me find them." Justin pointed his chin toward the backpack boy, who was now a healthy distance away. "Now go before you lose him. And *don't* lose him."

I groaned and dragged my feet as I walked in the direction of the backpack kid. What had I gotten myself into?

CHAPTER 6

MICHELLE

I wove through the crowd, my eyes ever on the mayor.

He wore a smart-looking red polo with shorts.

I watched his hands, waiting for them to slip into his pocket. They never did.

Still ... something didn't sit right. He'd turned in the theft, talked the details over with the police, then just walked away.

Why would he walk away?

Why not stay and help investigate?

Why not stick close to a police officer until he had the truth and his money returned?

I never would have walked away.

No, something didn't sit right.

The mayor paused on the edge of the grass and looked both ways.

I grinned to myself as I paused too, forever remaining at an unsuspicious distance.

He cut across the parking lot in a jog, slipping through two rows of cars before he stopped and let himself into one.

It was a newer model of something royal blue. And it didn't need a wash like mine did.

I stepped under a shade tree and held the phone to my ear, staring "leisurely" into the distance … and directly at the mayor.

It'd be near impossible to see his hands slip into his pockets and pull out the money from here, but I watched anyway.

His hands, however, gripped the steering wheel. The car turned on, but it didn't move. And other than starting the car, his hands remained on the wheel. Then he said something to himself.

I cut my eyes in both directions, but we were oddly alone out here.

He said something else, then laid his head down on the steering wheel between his hands. At once, he lifted his head.

I jolted, almost losing my grip on the phone.

But he didn't look at me. He looked at his ceiling and continued talking to himself.

Reality swept over me. This man was praying!

My heart pinched. Chelsea was right this time. The mayor wasn't guilty.

"Father, forgive me for jumping to conclusions." I turned away, leaving the mayor to his privacy.

Okay. The mayor was innocent, but someone else was sure guilty.

I stalled on the grassy hill, overlooking the park. Someone here stole the money.

I mentally walked through the suspects. The children in the distance looked like scrambling bugs, climbing on and off the playground equipment, soaking in the last of the day's sunlight.

The food trucks and Anderson grill were stationed close enough to tempt all the little tummies, plus those on the blanketed grounds. Harv had insisted on setting up an iced coffee stand this year. I had helped to set it up next to the snow cone truck earlier this morning.

Good guy that my co-owner was, he insisted that he'd man the stand since he didn't care as much for mingling with the people.

Conner's watermelon table was still in operation, but he wasn't working it.

"Enjoying yourself?" came a deep voice from behind me.

I spun around.

It was the mayor. He offered a smile, crinkling up the edges of his eyes. To everyone else, it might have just been a smile. But to me, I saw the fatigue and concern there.

"Yes, sir. Are you?"

He stood at my side and inhaled, taking in the crowds of people laid out in front of us. "It's one of my favorite times of the year. I love seeing the community come together in celebration, don't you?"

I grinned back at him. "I do. It's like a reunion with extended family."

His smile broadened. "I like that. Might even use it in my speech." He winked. "With your permission, of course."

"Use away."

He chuckled and stepped away, then turned back. "Don't hang back forever. Mix in there with your family."

"Yes, sir."

With a wave, he started down the hill without me.

I brushed across the canvas before me one more time and stopped short at the sight of Conner.

He put his hands on his hips.

I was too far away to see any hint of his inviting smile, but I could imagine it well enough.

He talked to a young woman. She gestured wildly with her hands.

My phone rang. Without looking, I slipped it from my pocket and answered.

"Shells, we have a situation here," Justin said in my ear.

"Well, I'm done with the mayor, so what do you need?"

"What happened with the mayor?"

"I'll explain later, but he's not our guy."

"Okay, well, Jenna showed me one of the contestants."

"Jenna?" Wasn't that Chelsea's job?

"Yeah, *I'll* explain later. But she pointed out Clarice. The angry loser."

"Yeah?"

"She's talking … to your watermelon guy."

A flash of something shot through my system. Excitement and hope. But also disappointment and unease. How did Conner factor into the theft? I didn't like the slew of possibilities that came to mind.

"I'm watching the two of them right now, actually. I didn't know who she was."

"Mm-hmm," he hummed sarcastically in my ear. "Well, I thought maybe you might want to give him another try."

"I can do that, but … I can't promise anything. After you scared him off, Kyle took a turn with him. I have a feeling he doesn't really want to talk to me anymore."

"Maybe. … Or maybe he has something to hide and *shouldn't* talk to you."

I grinned despite the nasty turn in my dating life. "I thought you were on flirting duty today."

He grunted. "Well, someone forgot to mention that this contest was for college students only. I'm nearly twenty years older than them."

I flicked a wrist. "College girls are notorious for falling in love with older men."

"Wrong. They fall in love with hunky college professors, not old strangers."

I laughed.

"Besides, you have a natural in with this guy, so I'm tagging you for flirting duty."

I didn't fight my grin. "Gladly."

"Hey, now," he growled in that older-brother way of his. "I'm watching you."

"Yeah, yeah." I hung up and scurried down the hill.

I walked straight for the pair.

Pair. I didn't know who Clarice was to him, but considering he was flirting with me when we first met, I was going to assume they weren't attached to each other.

Conner's eyes connected with mine.

I sent him an easy smile.

His eyes darted away, and he tried for something similar to a smile.

My gut dipped. He was far friendlier the first time we met. Justin might be right about him.

Justin. Crap. I forgot he was watching me.

I concentrated so hard on keeping my gait smooth that I was certain it was anything but smooth. I didn't know where my brother was, and I wasn't about to look around for him. He'd give me away for sure.

I tunneled a breath. I could do this.

I was just talking to the man. I wasn't the one potentially guilty of stealing anything. And I *had* wanted to talk to him.

I once again considered the connection we shared during our first meeting. Not to mention that smile, those eyes, and that beard.

Yep. I wanted to talk to this guy.

Okay. My mind was back in order. I stopped at the pair.

"Hey, Conner."

He shifted. "Hey, Michelle."

I cut my eyes to the girl.

"Oh, uh … This is my cousin, Clarice Jasper."

"Clarice …" I bit my lip in thought. "That name sounds familiar."

She watched me but said nothing.

"Were you …" I paused again, slowly connecting thoughts that Jenna had already put together for me. "Were you one of the finalists for the citizen award?"

She gave a nod, screwing her lips together.

Unexpected compassion swept over me. I reached for her shoulder and gave her a friendly squeeze. "You didn't win, did you?"

"No," she said quietly.

"I'm sorry, Clarice." And I meant it. The poor girl looked utterly defeated.

She flicked her eyes back to Conner, and a strong, proud smile emerged. "That's okay. I don't need the recognition or the prize money."

I worked not to show my surprise. "You're not sore about it?"

Clarice met Conner's eyes, a slow, confident smile appearing again. "Nope." She tilted her head to the side and gripped her purse straps at her shoulder with both hands. "I'm going to go visit with some friends." She pointedly looked at Conner. "Talk to you later?"

He nodded, then turned to me.

While Clarice radiated confidence, Conner looked drained of it.

Silence stretched between us.

He shifted again. He started to open his mouth, then closed it, his face darkening again.

"How are the watermelon sales today?"

"Great," he said in a rush. "Yeah, we sold more than expected. I had to … uhh … pick up some more. That's … where I was when you came by earlier."

I nodded along, but before I could think of what to say next, he took a step back.

"I should get back."

"Okay." I didn't try to stop him but watched him walk away.

I was heading back when Justin appeared at my side. "Bravo," he said. "I knew you could do it."

I didn't answer. I needed something crunchy to munch on to balance out the stress. Something crunchy … and cold. I swerved, circling around the snow cone line, to our coffee stand for four cups of crushed ice.

Harv sent me a wave over his head. "Having fun?"

"Yeah, you?"

"Best day ever!"

And his wide grin showed it too. Looks like putting up an iced coffee stand was the right move to make.

"Are you going to tell me what happened with the guy?" Justin asked.

I reached for the extended cups. "I'm still trying to process. Something isn't right, and I don't like it."

"But you like him?" He asked it like an accusation.

I lifted a shoulder.

We stepped away from the stand.

A little girl wrestled for control of the snow cone from her mother and it went flying in the air, landing on my feet.

I sucked in a squeal. Sticky ice slipped between my toes. I grimaced.

"I am so sorry!" The mother was suddenly in my face, her cheeks a cherry shade of red. The same shade as the melting ice at my feet, actually.

I tried to smile. "It's okay."

"Brandi, what happened?" her husband asked, rushing to her side with two more children.

Brandi looked ready to cry. "She dropped their snow cone."

The little girl was crying. The mom was nearly in tears. Little brother was starting to whimper, and the dad looked torn.

Justin leaned down to the little girl. "Accidents happen, don't they? How about we fix this one together?"

The little girl watched him with large blue eyes.

"What flavor was it?"

"Cherry," she whispered.

"You really don't–" the father started to say.

Justin rose and waved him off. "Don't worry about it. Let's just have a great day."

I beamed at my brother. He really would make a wonderful dad someday. He already made a top-notch brother and uncle.

"L-let's clean you up," Brandi said, coming back to life and her smile forming easier. She waved me over to a bench and sat down, drawing her giant diaper bag into her lap.

I watched as she unzipped the bag and began rifling through it.

She sent me a cautious look, pulling the bag closer to her chest and angling it away from me.

Taking the hint, I turned my head. What in the world was so private about diapers and wipes?

She whipped out a couple of wipes and handed them over to me.

I thanked her and cleaned my feet and shoes.

The men and children met us as I finished up.

"Thanks. That really does feel better."

"No problem. And I'm sorry, again."

I rose from the bench. "Don't worry about it." Pairing off with Justin, we walked away and left the little family behind.

"You're a really nice guy, you know?"

"You act surprised."

"No ... but I liked seeing it."

"You should have seen him!" some college girl screeched to her friend as they zipped right in front of us. "He actually asked me to go to some ritzy restaurant, like he has that kind of cash or something."

We pulled up short to miss being trampled by the teens so involved in their conversation that they failed to see anyone around them.

Her friend snorted. "I can't even."

"Neither can I!" I shouted at their backs.

Justin cut me a big brother look.

"What? Am I invisible today? I've been scratched, splashed, and now almost stepped on."

"You have had a time of it, huh?"

"Yeah," I said with a sigh.

After a moment passed, he asked, "Are you thinking about Watermelon Guy?"

"I thought we really connected."

He bumped me with his shoulder. "It'll happen again for you, Shells. Just be patient."

I tried to smile. Sure. I might fall in love again. But ... what would keep me from falling back out ... again?

I wasn't about to ask my brother that, and we were back at our chairs, so I dropped the conversation. I handed Chelsea a cup of ice, and Justin gave one to Jenna.

They thanked us, and we sank down on our chairs.

I swallowed a refreshing bite of ice. "Okay. Time to get down to business."

Chelsea shrank a bit in her chair.

"Come on, Sea," I said internally.

"Shells ..." my twin internally grumbled back.

"We're doing this," I insisted.

"But ..."

We stared at one another, neither speaking out loud.

"But nothing," I insisted.

"Fine."

"Okay," I said aloud, including Jenna and Justin in our conversation. "Our suspects. We thought the mayor was guilty–"

"You thought the mayor was guilty."

I sent my sister a tight smile. "Fine. *I* thought the mayor was guilty. But we can confidently cross him off our list. So–"

"Why?" Chelsea asked. "What aren't you telling us?"

I huffed. "I followed him to the parking lot. He locked himself in his car and prayed, then returned to the picnic."

"Ha! You see there! You see now how wild and unfounded your accusations are?"

"No, I don't," I said, sitting up straighter. "He could have been guilty."

"Anyone here could have been."

"Exactly."

She rolled her eyes. "Really, Shells, we should just move on with our day. It's not our business."

"We'll move on because we're almost done. Our list is getting shorter."

"Actually," Justin cut in, "it's getting longer." He slid his eyes to Chelsea. "Sea ..."

Chelsea shook her head. "You know what this will lead to."

"Tell her or I will."

"Tell me what?" I said, eying them both.

Chelsea rolled her eyes. "I remembered this college kid near the fire. But," she rushed on, "he was likely putting out the alleged fire like the other men were doing. But *your* brother insisted that I keep an eye on him."

"Really?" I grinned at her mention of *my* brother. It's always galled her how well Justin and I got along. Or maybe it was because we got into similar scrapes together. I dropped my legs down and leaned forward. "And what did you find?"

"Nothing. He talked to some girl. That's it."

"That's it?" I said with squinted eyes.

"That's it."

"He did have a backpack," Justin said between scoops of ice.

I chewed on this information and took another spoonful for myself. Turning to Jenna, I asked, "What did you learn?"

"Well, I checked in with my mom. She knows Alexis's family really well."

"And she's the one who won the contest, right?" I asked.

Jenna nodded. "Right. Her family is loaded. She's fully covered, never works, and has a regular allowance. She doesn't need the money." She cut her eyes to Chelsea and grimaced as if she hated playing along when it was clear my sister was being outnumbered. "I kept hearing how the other finalist, Clarice, was so angry about not winning. That makes sense because Clarice doesn't come from money and has to work while attending college."

I nodded. "So she's the one with the true motive."

"Of the two …" Jenna said with a wince, "I'd say Clarice has the most convincing motive."

"You know what's odd? She was talking to Conner, my watermelon guy."

"Your what?" Chelsea hissed.

I waved her off. "Cute guy, sells watermelon. I'll tell you about him later. I talked to her and Conner, and she was disappointed but not angry. She was actually … at peace."

"At peace?" Jenna and Chelsea said together.

"She was far from at peace when I overheard her earlier today," Chelsea said.

I hid my grin. I loved seeing my sister take an interest.

Jenna shook her head. "I've heard from multiple sources, some more reliable than others, that she was more than a little angry."

"Well, she's sure changed her tune." I leaned back again.

"Brandi, get her!"

A girlish giggle tore through our thoughts as the snow cone-dropping child tore across the lawn.

Her mom raced after her, clutching her flopping diaper bag at her side.

I watched the pair. "What do y'all know about that family?" I said with a tip of my head at the young couple and their children.

"Nothing, why?" Jenna asked.

"I ran into them earlier and something odd happened."

"Odd?" Chelsea asked. "Why is it that every odd thing is a crime with you?"

I sent her a snarky grin. "I'm just lucky, I guess."

She rolled her eyes in that big sister sort of way.

"I sat beside Brandi while she dug through her diaper bag, and she didn't like me seeing inside the bag."

"Okay?" Jenna said.

"A purse, I can understand. But a diaper bag?"

"A diaper bag is some women's purse," Chelsea said.

I watched the children's fleeting backs as they continued racing through the park. "Even then ... woman to woman, what's so personal in a purse? What do we carry?"

"I don't want to know," Justin said.

"Makeup and a wallet," Jenna said, ignoring Justin.

"Exactly. Pens, paper, and maybe some candy. Of course, our —"

"Don't," Justin stressed. "I didn't sign up for this abuse."

The three of us laughed at his male drama.

"*Personal* items aren't that personal among women."

"For some people, it is," Chelsea said.

"But for many, it isn't," Jenna said.

"But get this," I said, "I overheard her talking earlier today. They have a big vacation coming up."

Chelsea snorted.

I snapped to attention and openly studied her.

"I don't know them at all," Jenna said.

"Sea?"

"You know I can't–"

"Talk about customers," we finished together.

"Yeah, I know. But the idea of an expensive vacation surprises you, doesn't it?"

She turned her eyes away which said all I needed to know.

"Which means that an extra $500 could go a long way," Justin said.

"I didn't say that," Chelsea said.

Not saying anything was more than enough admission in my book.

"Well …" I said, looking at each of their faces. "What do we make of the evidence?"

Chelsea squirmed and dug into her cup of ice as if she could really hide in there.

I let her hide and flipped my gaze between Justin and Jenna. "Someone stole the money. Who do we think did it, and how do we prove it?"

CHAPTER 7

CHELSEA

It wasn't our responsibility to prove who stole the money. I fished out a piece of ice and let it melt for a few seconds in my fingers as I procrastinated bringing it to my mouth. If only I could melt Michelle's ideas as quickly and effortlessly.

"Are we taking a vote?" Justin asked. "Cause I vote for one of the chicks."

I studied my ice. If it would stop my siblings' discussion, I'd chuck it at them.

"Okay, okay…" Michelle rubbed her hands together. "Clarice and Conner…" She hesitated slightly at his name. "They're cousins. He left to supposedly restock his melons. She went from being mad at Alexis for winning to not really caring."

"Then there's the married chick," Justin took over.

"Brandi," I muttered.

He gave me a wink. "The married chick named Brandi."

I groaned. He was impossible.

"But would she really have an opportunity with three kids in tow?" I challenged.

Michelle snorted. "You're too soft. That just makes her *seem* like she has the perfect alibi. Let's not forget, she has an accomplice: her husband."

"Who is also toting around the other half of their family."

Michelle waved me off. "Still not impossible."

"But I didn't see either of them anywhere near the podium," I countered. "And maybe they were saving for the vacation with cash and change. It's fully possible."

"And then there's the college dude," Justin finished, as if Michelle and I hadn't said a word. He slid a sly glance at me. "Who was talking to a chick."

I clenched my teeth. If I stopped reacting, Justin would drop this little game he thought amusing.

"Well, we're not going to figure it out just by supposing," Jenna said matter-of-factly. "Any three of them could have a legitimate reason for stealing the cash. Our theories won't hold up in court."

Michelle snapped her fingers. "So we get them to show their hand."

"If they have a hand to show," I muttered. "Has the thought crossed your mind that maybe *none* of our suspects are actually guilty?"

"Psh!" Michelle and Justin reacted together.

They were too much alike sometimes.

Michelle scanned the crowd. It was starting to grow dusky, which meant the fireworks show would be soon.

"They've gotta still be here," Michelle said. "Kyle said no one's allowed to leave without being searched."

"It's not like the park is fenced in," I pointed out.

"This thief is confident," Michelle said. "They'll leave with the mass exodus. Which means we have about one and a half hours to figure this out."

"Or the police do." I added an extra emphasis to my words.

Michelle speared me with a glare. "That is getting *really* old really fast."

I threw up my hands, certain Michelle could read my thoughts loud and clear. I wouldn't have to keep saying it if she didn't have selective comprehension of my words.

"We need to lure them in…"

"No Scooby Doo scheme," I interrupted Michelle.

She froze and glared at me with more disappointment than anger this time. *"It would have worked,"* she said silently.

"Not a chance," I countered.

"Well," she said out loud, "we have to force one of them to the surface, and you're trying to make excuses for all of them."

"Legitimate, logical reasons," I corrected.

"Abby!" Panic laced a woman's voice as she called out the name.

All four of us turned toward the cry. It was Brandi. She rushed past our chairs, her eyes meeting ours briefly. Recognition flickered in her eyes. "Have you seen my daughter?"

"No, ma'am." Justin stood and took a step closer to her. "Her name is Abby?"

"Mhm." Brandi's gaze jerked around, scanning every small child.

"We'll help you find her," I volunteered. This was a much more worthy cause than Michelle's harebrained entertainment.

"Oh, thank you!" Tears filled Brandi's eyes. "Um, my phone number …" She slipped her diaper bag straps off her shoulder and started digging. "I can't ever remember it. I have business cards in here somewhere. It has both mine and my husband's numbers …"

"I'll help you," Michelle offered.

My devious little sister! I clenched my jaw to keep from glaring at her. But within thirty seconds, Michelle had the business cards out and in our hands and Brandi was gushing her thanks again before speeding off.

"Michelle Renee!" I hissed.

She gave me an innocent shrug. "One suspect down."

"And one girl to find." I stormed off before she could say anything else. *Lord, please help someone find Abby.* We should text Kyle. Surely he could spare half the force team to look for a girl instead of money. I glanced back to tell Michelle, but she already had her phone to her ear. Yep, she was calling him.

Justin jogged up behind me. "She was pretty crazy about those snow cones."

"Mhm … I heard her begging for them earlier. Do you think she went back for another one?" I hoped something that simple was the case.

"On a hot day like today, wouldn't you?"

"Yeah."

We pushed through the crowd to the snow cone stand just in time to see Brandi's husband kneel down and pull Abby into his arms. The girl let out a torrent of sobs.

"Apparently he had the same bright idea." Justin's face beamed with a smile of relief. "I think she deserves another snow cone."

"For running away?" I asked.

He gave me a sour look. "She's just a baby."

"Well, at least let the parents decide." I stepped forward and met Blake's eyes. "I'm so grateful you found her! We ran into Brandi. Do you want me to call her?"

Blake nodded as he tried to calm his daughter.

I thumbed Brandi's number into my phone. Brandi picked up on the first ring.

"Abby's with your husband," I said.

"Oh, praise God!" Tears clouded her voice.

"We're at the snow cone stand."

"Thank you so much!" She clicked off, and I heard Abby try to answer her daddy's question through broken sobs.

"I ... was just ... wanted to share ... with Jamie. But I accidentally ... didn't have any left. I didn't ... mean to ... lose you. I'm sorry, Daddy." More sobs threatened to pour out, and Blake whispered in her ear.

"Aw, she wanted to share it with her baby." Justin gave a pout.

Oh man. If he ever married and had a daughter, he would be one big softie.

"Ask the parent before she hears you," I mouthed in warning. I'd learned years ago to never get between a kid and the parent.

Abby's face was still buried in her dad's shoulder. Justin pulled out a $5 dollar bill and waved it toward Blake.

"I remember being a kid with little siblings," Justin said. "But I didn't want to share with them."

Blake studied the money flapping in Justin's hand.

"Please, I'm just so glad she's found. That is worth far more than this."

Blake gave a sigh.

Yep. Men and cute little girls. They were both suckers.

Justin presented the bill to the tear-streaked little girl, and we left the now-happy family in the snow cone line.

I texted Michelle and Jenna, and we gathered back at our seats.

"You can't ever say it's dull in Maple Springs," Michelle quipped. "One mystery solved, one more to go. And we're one step closer." Her eyes sparkled. "I'm pretty sure Brandi is ashamed of her homemade snacks and divvied-up baggies, and that's what she was hiding in her diaper bag."

"Why would she be ashamed of that? That was our life growing up." I'd never gotten my own little bag of chips unless it was in a baggy.

Michelle sniffed. "You don't know her *friends*. She should get new ones. Apparently they're snobs."

I didn't even ask how she knew.

The thud of the microphone interrupted us.

"Good evening, Maple Springs." The mayor's voice boomed across the park and the hubbub of conversation died down.

I caught Michelle looking at everything but the mayor. She caught my eye and gave a shrug and a wink.

After the mayor gave his welcome, he said, "And now, for one of the biggest events of the year, our Citizen's Award. I am pleased to announce Alexis Jones as this year's winner of the award and $500 cash prize." He went on voicing Alexis's accolades without a single hitch.

I turned to Michelle. Her eyes were fixated on a person. I knew even before I followed her gaze that it was Clarice.

"She's not angry," Michelle murmured.

An uneasy feeling tinged in my gut. "She doesn't look gleeful either."

"No …" At least Michelle agreed with me. Her pensive look told me she was trying to piece things together. "But she doesn't look altogether happy."

Her eyes darted to Alexis, who was beaming as she shook the mayor's hand.

"That's a tense smile if I ever saw one," Michelle said.

"Ya think?" Justin asked. "The prize money is still missing. I wonder if they scrounged up $500 or that tense smile is because she knows it's missing."

"Or because she stole it and her conscience is getting to her." Michelle looked between Alexis and Clarice.

I wasn't even going to follow that train of thought. Maybe the guilty person would confess without our involvement.

"Enjoy your family tonight, Maple Springs. In about forty-five minutes we'll end with the greatest fireworks show of the year!"

Everyone applauded, and Michelle bolted upright in her chair. "Clarice is approaching Alexis!"

At the same time, Justin laid a hand on my shoulder. "Hey, Sea ..." His voice was semi-absent as he studied someone in the distance. "That's the college guy you saw, right?"

I followed his gaze. It was the same tall, lanky kid with glasses and curly brown hair. "Yeah."

"Shells ... is that the girl who nearly ran you over?"

Michelle jerked her attention away from Alexis and Clarice and squinted. "Yeah." Her gaze went immediately back to the duo.

"Do you remember what she said?"

"I was kinda too busy trying not to be trampled. I didn't have time to be nosy."

"That's a first," I muttered.

Michelle shot me a look, but we both dissolved into giggles before she turned her focus back on Alexis and Clarice.

"Well, that was anticlimactic." Michelle slumped back in her chair. "Apparently Clarice congratulated her with a hug."

I bit back an I-told-you-so.

Justin interrupted my thoughts. "She was saying something about being asked out to a ritzy restaurant and didn't know how he had the cash."

It took me a second to register that he hadn't followed our scenic route away from the college boy and his girlfriend wanna-be.

"Really?" Michelle stood up and joined Justin in staring. "She did, didn't she ..."

"Sea, what did you see with him at the fire?" Justin asked.

"Smoke bomb," I corrected. Then added, "He was coming out of the smoke …"

Michelle spun to me. "Are you kidding me?"

"What? He was probably just putting what he thought was the fire out."

"Did you *see* him helping?" Michelle probed.

"Well, no …"

"So what *did* you see? Think. Did he have a cup or a water bottle he could have used to help?"

I closed my eyes and replayed the scene. "He was just walking out of the smoke. He was coughing and struggling to breathe. I gave him some water, and he pulled out an inhaler."

"Wait. He had an inhaler with him?"

"Yeah. So?"

"Why would he even be *in* the smoke if he knew it would give him an asthma attack?" Her eyes lit with excitement. "He would only be *in* there if *he* was the one who set the fire and stole the money!" She spun toward the college kid.

"No …" I grappled for her arm and clung to it. "There were lots of people running around there."

"But you already said that he didn't have anything in his hands to help put out the fire."

"That doesn't mean–"

"How many others were there helping out?"

"I don't know. A few."

"So more than one, which means he didn't *have* to be there. But he was. You didn't see him with any sort of liquid container."

"He could have dropped it."

"Did he? Were there any bottles of water or cups laying around back there?" Michelle glanced at everyone, but Justin and Jenna only shook their heads. "I think he's our guy."

"No, no, no. He … was probably …"

"You can't keep thinking everyone is innocent!"

"And you can't keep thinking everyone is guilty. Just a few minutes ago you were convinced it was Brandi, an hour ago you were convinced it was the mayor. And not five minutes ago, you were still watching Alexis and Clarice. Not everyone is guilty."

"Not everyone is innocent either."

"Okay, okay!" Jenna spoke up, interrupting our quarrel. "I'm with Justin on this one. The guy had means, motive, and opportunity. But ... what can we do about it?"

"Tell Kyle," I said at the same time Michelle spouted off, "Corner him."

I glared at her. "If we spook him, Kyle's gonna be on *your* case."

"I agree," Justin said with a voice of authority he rarely used. "If he's our guy, it would go a lot better if we didn't get in the way and tamper with evidence."

"Psh, Kyle won't listen to me," Michelle said.

I bit my tongue before I said, *I wonder why.* But the look Michelle gave me said she heard my thoughts loud and clear.

"I'm not volunteering," Jenna said.

"I'll do it." Justin looked as if it would be a great pleasure to do so. "Man to man, he'll listen to me."

Or so we hoped.

Michelle muttered something under her breath. I didn't want to know what it was, but I was pretty sure it was slanted against Kyle being difficult to work with.

"I'll keep an eye on the kid then." Michelle proved her point by gluing her eyes to him.

"He hasn't moved in the five minutes we've been watching him," I said. He clearly was engrossed in wooing his girl.

"But he might. Run, get Kyle." Michelle shoved Justin as she took a few steps toward the college kid, pulling out her phone to mask her surveillance.

I watched, but from a much safer and less-nosy distance. Not that it didn't make me feel guilty.

A ball rolled into the college boy's foot. He stopped talking and looked down at it, then glanced around. A smile brightened his face as he bent down and picked it up.

He shouted something, then the ball sailed smoothly to a little kid. The kid waved, and the college boy waved back, fidgeted with his glasses, and resumed talking to the girl.

My stomach clenched as I saw an officer in the distance walking toward the college boy. I scanned the crowd and spotted another officer. Then Kyle.

Justin rejoined our group and nodded toward the officers as if I hadn't already seen them.

What if we were wrong?

Correction–what if Michelle was wrong? I didn't want to be a part of this.

Michelle was shuffling backwards to us, her eyes not leaving the college kid. "So he believed you?"

"You didn't doubt he would, did you?" Justin asked.

"Did you tell him about the inhaler and asthma attack?"

"Yes, Shells."

"What did he ask us to do?" Michelle didn't take a seat. In fact, I was pretty sure she'd start sprinting in the next second if Justin gave the command.

"Nothing."

Michelle pouted. "I could make Kyle's job easier. Lure him in …" Her eyes darted to the scene unfolding.

The college boy was still talking to the girl, his hand secure on his backpack strap. The closest officer was still yards away, but striding closer. Just one minute now …

"I hope you're right," I muttered.

"Oh, I am." Michelle oozed with confidence, but there was a slight hitch in her breath that made me wonder if she was second-guessing herself too.

Thirty seconds.

"The poor girl if we are right," Jenna whispered.

"She'll know not to date a jerk," Michelle said. "Oh! He just saw them."

Sure enough, the college kid shifted his backpack as his eyes darted from one officer to the other. The girl frowned at him, as if puzzled.

The college boy gripped his backpack straps and ran. Straight in our direction.

CHAPTER 8

MICHELLE

The little creep was going to run.

If that didn't spell his guilt, I don't know what did.

I shot a glance at Kyle who fixated on his target, starting out in a jog as the boy picked up speed.

"Shells, don't," Chelsea called.

She might as well have said "Do it," because the second he came close enough, I launched at him, driving my shoulder into his side.

We tumbled to the ground together.

He bellowed.

I screamed as I tangled with his backpack, then slid down his chest, hitting the ground.

If this dude was innocent, I was going to look like the biggest idiot.

I rolled onto my back. Officer Adam hovered over me, then Officer Rob.

Kyle was panting, leaning over me next. "Shells, are you okay?"

I sent him a tired grin and nodded.

"Why did you do that? We were on him."

I smirked, then groaned. "No one likes to run in this heat."

Officer Adam chuckled.

The two men pulled the boy to his feet.

Kyle reached for me.

I lifted both of my hands, but pain shot through my shoulder. With a gasp, I clutched it.

He frowned.

I sat up slowly, my gaze darting to the people–the many, many people–now gawking at us.

Man, this dude better be guilty.

I accepted Kyle's help with my good hand and rose to my feet.

"Are you okay?" he whispered, the softness in his voice betraying the stern look he had been giving me.

I rolled my shoulder. "Yeah. I don't think anything's broken."

I turned my attention back to the men in time to hear the boy state his name.

"Garret Allen, sir."

I held my breath, waiting to see if my heroic actions were for a good cause or if I had an apology and free lunch to hand out.

Beside me, Kyle shifted, still prime for action.

Officer Rob spoke to Garret about searching his bag.

I dusted myself off with my good hand. Maybe if I didn't make a sound, Kyle would forget I was here and let me stay.

Garret muttered a response, barely meeting either of the officers' eyes. He avoided mine altogether.

Guilty. An innocent man would be foaming at the mouth for being drilled into the dirt needlessly by a stranger.

I slid a glance to the girl he had been talking to.

She stared at the scene, color gone from her face, her finger in mid-twirl around a lock of hair from her ponytail.

Officer Rob reached into the backpack, shuffling content around.

He whipped out a lighter and handed it to Officer Adam. "Is this yours?"

Garret mumbled that it was.

Rob glanced at the other two officers, the three of them exchanging knowing looks.

"Do you smoke?"

"No, he has asthma," I said.

Every eye fell on me. Drat. I was about to get kicked out.

Adam bit back a grin.

Kyle edged me back by my elbow. "You just can't help yourself, can you?"

I winced, but only because I was being forced to leave.

Rob reached in and pulled out a gray metal box.

I gasped, rooted in place.

Kyle dug out a key from his pocket.

The mayor must have given it to him when I wasn't looking.

Rob slid it into the keyhole without a hitch and opened the lid.

We all stared in wonder at the missing money.

I exhaled the breath I had been holding.

"Good job, Snoopy," Kyle whispered. He pulled again on my elbow, and this time I went willingly.

Chelsea darted over to us. "Are you okay?"

I grinned from ear to ear. "Much better now."

She slapped my arm.

"Ouch!"

"What is the matter with you? Why couldn't you let the police handle it?" Her questions came out in a breathy whisper.

I sent Kyle a wounded look. "Kyle."

He shook his head. "I'm with her on this one."

Figures. On anything important, he always took her side.

"Were you trying to give me a heart attack?" he hissed, picking up her case.

"No." I smiled. "I was helping."

He sent me one of those looks, but I only smiled wider. It wasn't but a couple of hours ago he had accused me of impeding the investigation. "I totally 'peded' that investigation."

He snorted.

"Go ahead. Say it."

"Not happening," he said, his tone lighter than the scowl. He pointed with his head. "Why don't the two of you go sit down?" He gave my back a gentle pat in parting. He wasn't half as angry as he tried to be.

Chelsea was already pulling on my good arm.

"And stay out of trouble," he hollered over his shoulder at us.

Justin met me with a bear hug, Jenna trailing behind him. "That's my little sister!"

I pushed out of his hold. "Careful. You're hurting me."

"Sorry. I can't believe you. What were you thinking?"

"She wasn't," Chelsea grumbled, sinking into her seat.

I giggled. "I wasn't thinking about much. I just … knew he couldn't get away. And I also knew he wouldn't be expecting me."

"He will be from now on."

We all laughed, and even Chelsea cracked a grin.

I knew she loved me. If she loosened up a bit, she might even admit that she loved being a part of solving this. She just worried too much.

I watched as Rob steered Garret through the crowds. Poor guy didn't even put up a fight. I didn't know if he was still in shock over my tackle or if he just knew he was caught red-handed and there was nothing he could do.

The girl he had been talking to stood with her friends, still staring wide-eyed in disbelief.

Love made you do stupid things. I kinda felt bad for him. I popped an ice cube in my mouth and sucked on it.

Justin walked over to Kyle and Adam.

Kyle placed his hands on his hips, sweat beading his brow.

I turned, eyeing our seating arrangement. "Sea? Do we have any more bottles of water?"

"There's one left. But it's warm by now." Before I could ask her where it was, she added, "I slipped one in your purse for you."

I grinned at my sister for knowing me so well and went for the bottle. Twisting it open, I poured it into my half-filled ice cup and headed for Kyle. By the time I reached him, Adam walked away.

I extended the cup to Kyle as I stopped in front of him.

Kyle glanced down at the cup, then back up at me with a question in his eyes.

"Drink," I commanded.

"I'm not thirsty."

I huffed and wiggled the cup. "You always do this."

"Do what?" he asked, his voice hitting a higher note.

"Over-fixate on something and forget to stay hydrated."

"I do not."

Chelsea and Jenna completed our circle with their own ice cups in their hands.

"When was the last time you drank something?"

"I had something earlier."

I tilted my head in emphasis. "When? My sugary snow cone?"

"Maybe. I'm fine."

"Wait," Justin said, making a time-out signal with his hands. "Time out." He waved his finger between the two of us. "Did the two of you break up or get married? Because I'm confused."

We both glared at him.

I rolled my eyes and turned back to Kyle. "There's no way you're fine."

"I think I know whether or not I'm okay."

"Oh, come off it, Kyle. It's hotter than blazes out here, you're sweating, and you're wearing all this extra weight," I said, gripping the edge of his bulletproof vest at his armhole and giving it a jerk, but the large man didn't budge. My hand came away wet. "Eww," I whined, reluctantly wiping my hand on my hip.

Kyle smirked as if he had been sweating buckets just for this very moment.

"You're *sweating*," I stressed again. "You need to drink something."

"I would, but I'm fine."

"Shells," Chelsea moaned.

I ignored her. "Fine? Wow, really? Okay. We'll see how fine you are when you pass out from dehydration. They'll have to call the paramedics, you know? Boy, won't that be embarrassing to see our big strapping hero laid out in the dirt, receiving medical care? I'll try not to say I told you so, but I think we both know that I will anyway."

"Give me the cup," he grumbled, snatching it out of my hand. He gulped once, then twice before a look of satisfaction hit his face.

I grinned.

He smiled back sheepishly. "Okay, that does feel good."

"You think?"

"Seriously!" Justin shouted. "Did I miss the wedding?" He eyed Chelsea and Jenna. "Am I the only one seeing this?"

"Nope," Jenna said softly, tucking her smile away.

Chelsea eyed each of us. "Some of us are just used to it, I guess."

I met Kyle's eyes.

"He's your brother," Kyle whispered with a smirk.

"Don't remind me."

"But what is all this?" Justin asked, staring expectantly at us both.

"It's called friendship."

"Friendship?"

"Yeah," I said sarcastically. It was just like my lunatic brother to act like he didn't understand how to be a decent human being.

"So if the rest of us stopped drinking, you'd force water down our throats?"

I shrugged. "Sure, if I wanted to keep you alive. But you probably shouldn't test my affections today."

Kyle sent me a tight smile. "I better go. Thanks for the water."

After Kyle walked away, Justin zeroed in on me. "What. Was. That?"

I sent Chelsea a pleading look.

She winced, grabbed Jenna's arm, and sped away.

I turned back to Justin.

"Oh, I'm not going anywhere until I get some answers."

I squirmed under my big brother's scrutiny. Justin was my pal. My partner in crime. But when it came to guys ... he was my big brother. Being nine years older than us came with a particular level of protectiveness.

"Are the two of you ... casually dating or something?"

"No, I swear, we really are just friends."

"Then what was all that about?"

"We're *great* friends." I winced. "He's my best friend, aside from Chelsea. Just because we're not dating anymore, doesn't mean I don't know or understand him."

He exhaled. "So you still ... look out for each other?"

"Yeah."

Around us, families were settling into their seats or on their blankets. The sunlight was fading faster now that it had started.

"Maybe we should go sit down," I said, hoping he'd take the hint.

He didn't. It was Justin, after all. "Shells?"

I hesitated, then met his eyes. "Yeah?"

"What's going on?"

"I already told you, we're–"

"Friends. Yeah, I get it. But … why?"

"Why what?" I could hardly breathe. Surely, Justin didn't think there was something wrong with us remaining friends. It was hard enough to set Kyle aside as a boyfriend, but losing him as a friend would be too much. I needed him. He was my rock. My center.

He was my best friend.

Justin started and stopped twice before finally spitting out, "Why aren't the two of you together?"

My stomach twisted. It was that dreaded question again. I hardly knew why we weren't together, only that something was off between us. But I couldn't exactly deny that something was wonderfully right between us too. It hardly made sense to me either, and I was terrified at every moment that I was making the biggest mistake of my life. But the thought of getting back together made me hyperventilate. Which was crazy really. Kyle was the image of safety.

"Where does Watermelon Man fit into all of this?"

I shrugged. "I'm moving on."

He snorted. "Are you?"

I walked away.

"Shells," he moaned, catching up to me.

"Stop, Justin. I'm done talking about this."

"Fine." He tugged on my arm, and I stopped to face him. "Just … don't wait forever to change your mind. … And it *is* okay to change your mind."

I didn't say anything in return. The painful reality was that I hadn't changed my mind, and it didn't make a lick of sense to me either.

We made our way back to our seats in silence.

I pulled my seat closer to Chelsea's and sank down.

"Are you okay?" she mouthed.

I gave a slight nod.

My shoulder throbbed. I looked around for my purse.

Beside me, Chelsea read a text message. "Coconut, Mocha, or Vanilla?"

"Huh?"

She grinned. "Jenna is grabbing you a cup of coffee. Those are the flavors Harv has left out here. Which do you want?"

I beamed. Chelsea knew me too well. "Coconut."

Chelsea texted my response, then looked up at Justin. "Do you want anything?"

He shook his head, concerned eyes grazing me.

I fished out some pain pills and took them with my coffee after Jenna returned. Still uncomfortable, and not just because of the pain swelling in my shoulder, I pulled out my cell phone and shot Justin a text. "I love you."

He sent a winky face back.

I smiled and set my phone in my lap.

A boom interrupted the night and color exploded in the sky.

There was a collective inhale across the park at the sudden shock, but you never heard it again as blast after blast shook the quiet and stole our imaginations.

I inched my chair closer to my sister and leaned on her shoulder.

She returned the gesture and rested against my head.

My phone vibrated in my lap. I opened it.

Justin had sent a picture of me and Chelsea from behind us, fireworks exploding in the sky above our heads. The caption read, "My sissies."

I smiled, batting back the rush of tears. I wiggled my fingers to get her attention. "Look at your phone."

She did. "Aww." She texted back heart emojis.

Suddenly, fireworks started overlapping each other in rapid, machine-gun-fire bursts, flooding the sky with red, white, and blue cascades of color. When it was over, an awed hush fell over everyone.

We cheered with the crowd, then rose and stretched.

I took a sip of my coconut latte and froze.

Kyle stood laughing with Alisson Parker.

I watched the two of them, a swell of discomfort rising in my chest.

He didn't have the mannerisms of a kind stranger. He wasn't rigid like when he's working. He was … simply a guy enjoying the company of a woman.

My eyes watered again, which was ridiculous. Then again, maybe not so unreasonable considering the day I had. My emotions had a mind of their own when I grew too tired.

I felt Chelsea's presence beside me.

She snaked her arm around me and squeezed.

I smiled. "She's a nice girl."

Chelsea watched me, waiting.

"I'm fine, Sea." I turned to her, meeting the question in her eyes that I knew without looking would be there. "Honest. It was time."

She blinked.

"I like Kyle. And I like Alisson. They make sense." I smirked. "I don't like change, so there's that. But … I can get on board with this."

Finally she smiled.

Jenna walked up, then reared back, eyes locked on Kyle and Alisson.

"What are we—" Justin said. "Oh …"

Jenna stepped back.

"I'm with you, sister," he muttered and followed after Jenna.

77

Once we were alone again, Chelsea found her voice. "Are you really okay?"

"Yeah." My stupid eyes watered even more. I laughed because I couldn't control it anymore than I could control the weather. "It's weird," I said, my voice hitting a squeaky note. "But ... I like weird. It's fine."

"Shells."

"Sea." My chin wobbled. "I'm just tired. Honest. I think if he'd told me, I would have been better. But I wasn't expecting to turn around and see him smiling at some chick, you know? But ... it's okay. I mean ... I really don't want to get back together. I just ... man, I hate change, you know?" With an awkward laugh, I wiped my eyes.

Chelsea nodded along, but I knew she didn't get it. How could she? I didn't get it. Maybe ... maybe Chelsea was right before in what she said about not deciding my relationship with Kyle based on feelings. Because on paper we made the most sense in the world.

I turned away, needing something else to do, and gathered up my things.

Chelsea did likewise.

"Hey," a masculine voice said on Chelsea's other side.

"Hey," she said in her awkward, "why-are you-talking-to me" tone.

There was Kyle, smiling at some chick. Then there was Chelsea, shutting down anyone who approached her.

I laughed to myself and folded up the lap blanket.

"Did you enjoy the show?" the man asked.

"Yeah," my sister said simply.

"Look ... uh ... I'm real sorry about what happened earlier. I ... should have heard you out. And–"

"Whoa, hang on. Michelle?"

"Yeah?"

She sighed with relief. "I think someone is trying to talk to you."

I peered around her. "Conner! Hi."

His mouth fell open, and he stared at the two of us. He shifted nervously.

I looped an arm around Chelsea. "I see you've met my twin sister, Chelsea."

"Twins?" he repeated.

I smiled wider. "Identical."

He swallowed and looked around at everything except us.

"Chelsea said you wanted to talk to me."

"Yeah, uhh." He cleared his throat. "Mom explained the situation between you and your brother ... and your cop ... friend."

"Yyyesss?"

"I'm really sorry. ... That I didn't hear you out the first time."

"Apology accepted."

"Hey, hey," Justin boomed, walking up to us. "Watermelon man! You've got some great watermelon, dude."

"Thanks."

"You remember my brother, Justin."

Justin winked at me and threw his hands up. "Don't worry, I'll behave this time."

I sent Conner a look. "Don't believe him. I'm not sure he knows how."

Justin caught my eye. "I'm about to leave. Are you riding home with Sea?"

"Yeah. As long as she knows." I peered back.

Chelsea lifted a hand. "Heard you." Then she went back to folding up chairs. Jenna helped her slide them back into their pouches.

"I'll get moving," Justin said. "Thanks for inviting me."

"Thanks for coming."

He gave me another big hug and kissed my forehead. "Behave yourself. And don't tackle anyone else."

I winced. "Oh, I won't for a long time, trust me."

He laughed, then gave Chelsea the same bear hug and kiss treatment. He waved to Jenna.

"Tell everyone we said hello," Chelsea and I said together.

"And that we love them," Chelsea added.

"And give them a kiss for us," I added afterward.

Justin turned around and waved both hands in a shove-off manner. "Your message is too long. You'll have to come tell them yourself."

Laughing I turned back to Conner. "Sorry about that."

His smile came easier. "It's fine."

Clarice stopped at his side. "I'm heading home. I just wanted to say thank you again. I feel a lot better now."

He gave her a hug, pride swelling on his face. "You're welcome. Remember: these things aren't accidents, and you can trust God with them."

She smiled and nodded, then turned and disappeared into the crowd.

Conner shoved both hands into his pockets and sent me another shy grin. "Would you … uhh … like to come tour the farm sometime?"

There was a fluttering in my chest. This is what moving on felt like. I smiled freely. "I'd love to."

Confidence grew in his eyes, but he didn't say anything right away.

"Would you like my number?"

He jerked, coming to life, and digging out his phone. "Yeah."

I giggled and gave it to him.

He said goodbye and darted upstream through the crowd and back to his family's station.

I met Chelsea's eyes.

She sent me a loaded look.

Jenna laughed. "You've been quite busy today. Solving crime, tackling bad guys, and getting phone numbers."

I grinned at Jenna, then looked back at Chelsea.

She still didn't say anything. Her concern and disapproval radiated off of her.

I winked at my sister. "All in a day's work."

Chelsea gave a tired smirk. "Well, you're wearing me out with your day's work. Can we go home now?"

I closed the space between us and squeezed her.

She returned the hug.

"I love you," I whispered into her hair.

Her hold tightened. "I love you back."

We separated.

"Are you ready?"

I nodded, eyes grazing our fellow townspeople. *Thank you, Lord, for our home.* "Yeah, I'm ready."

I picked up one of the chairs, slinging it with my bag over my good shoulder, and thought of Kyle, Alisson, and Conner. I was ready for anything.

DATES WE QUESTION

MICHELLE

"Kyle?" I said breathlessly from my open front door.

Behind him, Conner stood outside of his truck, a look of indecision on his face. He had texted a minute ago to say he was here, so I dashed through my room, slipped on my shoes, and raced for the door.

Never in a million years did I expect Kyle to be standing at my door, hand already on the knob, keys dangling from the lock. He must have gotten here right before Conner.

Kyle sent me a tight smile, his cheeks as red as mine felt.

I opened my mouth to speak, but nothing came out.

We stared at each other, still caught in the doorway.

I exhaled, shoulders slumping.

Kyle swallowed but didn't speak.

"Is it too late to pretend to be Chelsea?" I whispered.

"Yeah," he whispered back.

My stomach knotted. I cast another look at Conner, who watched our every move.

Closing my eyes to them both, I tried to breathe again. "I didn't know how to tell you that I had a date." Opening my eyes, I met Kyle's.

"I get it … but … why didn't you at least tell me you were going out when I said I was coming over?"

"What are you talking about?"

"I texted you about twenty minutes ago and said that I was coming over. And you said, 'Sounds great. I'll see you soon.'"

I wanted to throw up. "Oh, Kyle, I am so sorry. I had been texting Conner this afternoon and thought it was him. I was a … bit distracted, getting ready."

His mouth hung open and he nodded. "Yeah, you look …"

The rest of that compliment was left dangling in the humid summer afternoon.

"I feel terrible."

Kyle winced. "No, don't. It was just a misunderstanding. I … uhhh," he said, shifting, "had been talking to Alisson some."

"Yeah," I said too quickly and far too high-pitched for normal conversation. But there was nothing normal about this. I mean … it was about to be normal, I suppose. But going on a date with someone new for the first time and actually having to do it in front of your ex … well, we deserved every awkward moment this was turning into. Normal couldn't return soon enough.

A door slammed.

Conner sat in his truck.

"I better go," I whispered.

Kyle jumped out of the way. "Yeah, of course."

I sped past him and down the steps.

"And I'm sorry," he called out.

"Me too, and, ummm. Sea will be here soon."

Now it was his turn to get high-pitched. "Yeah, great. I'll … uhh … just work on that puzzle for y'all."

I smiled and nodded. My stomach tightened as I hastened to the passenger side of Conner's truck. Opening the door, I pulled myself into the seat.

His AC blasted on my bare arm. "Sorry about that."

Conner continued staring out of his windshield. He turned up his hands, letting them fall back into his lap. "If you have other plans–"

"No, I don't. It was a miscommunication, that's all."

He looked at me, his brows hovering low.

I stared back into his warm brown eyes. How could I ruin this so soon? Chelsea would have a field day. I blew out a breath. "I … well … I don't even know what to say."

"Why is he letting himself into your house?"

"Well … he …" Geeze, this wasn't going to go any better.

"Does he live here or something?"

"No!" I touched his arm. "Oh, no, no, nothing like that at all. I swear. He's a good friend. Has a spare …" I gestured to my door, "and uses it when he comes over. It saves us from going to the door."

He flipped his gaze back to my front door where Kyle had disappeared.

"He was just coming to hang out. My sister will be here soon. … He's friends with both of us."

Conner nodded. "If you'd rather stay home–"

"No, please." I laid my hand on his arm again. "I want to go, I promise."

He studied me for a moment. "Okay." He put the truck in reverse and backed out onto the road, letting a tense silence settle between us.

I buckled and watched the familiar scenery pass by.

Without a word, he parked at the local diner.

"I thought we were going to your farm?"

"We are. I wanted to pick up some picnic food for us."

I smiled, a sweet warmth fanning over me. "Oh, that's nice."

He nodded. "Do you want to stay in the truck? I can leave it running for you?"

"No, it's fine. I'll come out with you."

He nodded again. Turning the engine off, he got out and started for the door.

I scrambled out to catch up.

He didn't wait for me, but pulled the door open and started through it. A second later, he stepped back out and held it for me.

I grinned back at him, whispering a thank you.

He didn't meet my eyes.

The slight sunk hard and fast in my middle. I blinked away a rush of emotion and watched from behind as Conner strode up to the counter without me.

Lord, help me fix this.

"Which one is she?" a gruff male voice asked in a whisper that wasn't quite low enough to be a real whisper.

"How should I know?"

"Don't you know?"

"No. Do you?"

"I wouldn't have asked you if I did."

I turned to the table where two older men talked.

They froze and stared back at me.

One by one, they grinned.

"Hi, dear."

I found a real smile for one of my sweet regulars. "Hi, Georgie. Hi, Arnold."

"Hi, …"

"Michelle," I filled in.

Georgie snapped his fingers. "I knew it."

"Did not," Arnold argued.

I giggled.

"Take a load off," Arnold said, shoving a chair away from the table.

I cast a look at Conner, who kept his back to me, then sat down. Minutes passed before Conner's shadow fell over me.

"We can leave now," he said.

I rose.

"What's the hurry?" Georgie said.

Conner's face darkened, but he didn't say anything.

I sent them both a teasing, scolding look. "We're–"

"Have an outing to get to," Conner slipped in.

Mischief, pure and simple, shone in their eyes.

I tried to laugh at their teasing looks and ignore the cold vibes from Conner.

"Well, if your *outing* isn't all it's cracked up to be, you know where to find us," Arnold said with a laugh.

I grasped both of their hands at once. "I'll keep that in mind. Now behave. Both of you."

"I ain't promising nothing," Georgie said to my back.

Conner pushed the door open and held it with his body.

I passed through and tossed a wave back at the men.

Again, I walked to my side of the truck alone and let myself in. The aroma of the food filled the cab of the truck as soon as he shut us inside.

"Smells good. What did you order?"

He lifted a shoulder. "A little of this, little of that."

My phone burned in my pocket. This outing was going nowhere fast. I considered calling Chelsea or Kyle for a ride home. But it took us a little while on the 4th to get our footing, so maybe a little more time would do us some good.

We drove fifteen minutes out of town before he turned us down a dead-end street.

If I didn't already know where their farm was, I would be reaching for my mace, but I knew I was safe.

I eyed the vast farmland. I hoped I was safe.

He pulled up close to a large farmhouse.

Two cars already sat in the wide gravel driveway.

His mom stepped out on the porch as we got out of the truck. She smiled warmly at me, and I soaked up the gesture. Turning to

Conner, she said, "I have the rest of your basket ready. It's inside when you want it."

He gave her a stiff nod.

She eyed him but didn't say anything.

A young woman stepped out onto the covered porch, holding a little boy nearly a year old. I recognized them both as customers from the shop, but I never had the chance to actually talk to them.

He was the cutest little boy, with black curly hair. I hadn't met his father, but he was certainly a dark man, making the boy a beautiful shade in between his parents.

"Who is that handsome boy?" I squealed, clapping my hands, eyes locked on the baby. There was something about this little guy that made me ache to scoop him up, squeeze, and love on him forever and ever.

"Don't be offended, honey; he doesn't take to strangers well," Conner's mom said. "But that's Aiden, my grandson."

There was such pride in her voice, which was no surprise. He was a cutie.

I drew closer and clapped my hands at him, grinning from ear to ear.

He laughed and leaned forward, almost diving out of his mother's arms.

She chuckled and readjusted him. "Well, look at you, trying to make friends for a change."

"Can I?" I asked, reaching for the little tyke.

"Of course."

I scooped him into my arms and squeezed him, kissing his plump cheek. Finally! "Hey, big boy. I finally got you. What do you think of that?"

Conner's mom laughed. "That's unexpected."

Not to me. I knew it was love at first sight the moment I saw him several months ago. "We're destined to be friends. That, and I'm not a *complete* stranger. I've never held him, but I've seen him plenty." Smiling at the mother, I said, "I'm Michelle Watson, by the way."

"I'm Rachel Sanders. I knew you were one of the twins, but I wasn't sure of your names or how to tell the two of you apart."

I laughed. "Very few people can tell us apart, so don't worry."

"Are you identical?" Conner's mom asked with a new sparkle of curiosity.

"Yes, ma'am."

"Your sister works at the bank, right?" Rachel asked.

"Yeah. Her name is Chelsea."

"Chelsea and Michelle. Okay. Got it. I think I can remember that. Then at least I can remember which one is which, pending on where I see you. If I catch you at the grocery store, I'm doomed."

"Don't worry. It happens to us all the time." Remembering Conner's recent mixup, I slid a glance at him, catching his silent study.

Conner's mom asked, "Where do you and Rachel see each other?"

"At the coffee shop," Rachel said.

She was a regular customer although until now I didn't know her name or that she was Conner's sister.

Conner snorted.

"Is there a problem?" Rachel asked, propping her hand on her hip.

"I can't believe you'd waste your money on overpriced coffee, is all," he grumbled.

She sent him a shocked look, then turned to me.

I gave a discreet shake of my head, then showered Aiden with kisses, sending him giggling.

"I hate to take him from his new friend, but we need to leave. We're meeting Dadda for dinner," she said cooing at him.

I handed him over and tickled his tummy. "Bye, buddy."

Aiden sent me a mournful look.

I waved, offering him a brave smile, then turned back to Conner, who was exchanging looks with his mom.

I couldn't read into their silent conversation, but given the things Chelsea and I said to each other silently, I wasn't sure I wanted to know what they were saying.

"I'll just grab the rest of our stuff, then we'll go," Conner said emotionlessly.

"Okay," I said lightly.

His mom sent me a sympathetic smile.

Before I could think of anything to say to fill yet another awkward silence, Conner returned. He motioned with his head for me to follow him, then started down the porch steps.

I whispered bye to his mom and scurried to catch up.

Up ahead was a large white building. A tractor sat in front of it. It must have housed other equipment, because it was too clean to keep animals.

"Do you want me to carry anything?"

"No, I got it." He trudged forward.

"Meow."

I hung back.

Without looking back, Conner called out, "Don't bother. He likes about two people."

The orange cat rubbed against a large rock outlining the walkway. He peered up at me and meowed again.

I intended to pass by him as Conner suggested, but if he was going to look at me that way, how could I? I held out my hand and drew closer. When he didn't run away, I eased closer until I could run my fingertips across the top of his head.

He leaned into my touch, so I knelt and scratched him more thoroughly.

"Aren't you a sweet boy?"

He started purring, so I scooped him up and nuzzled his head with my nose, scratching his neck.

"Mich–"

I stood and turned to Conner, who gaped at me.

After placing the bags on the tractor seat, he threw his hands up. "I give up."

"I'm sorry, I couldn't resist him."

He chuckled. "And he clearly couldn't resist you." Conner reached out to pet the cat but drew his hand back and huffed. "Just like my shy nephew, grumpy old men, ex-boyfriends, and any other man in your path, apparently. You're like a magnet or something."

"Umm. Okay." My stomach tightened. Was this supposed to be a compliment? It almost sounded like one except that his tone said he was more frustrated about it all.

The cat eyed him, then rubbed his head under my chin and leaned into my body.

"I thought I wanted to get this date over with, the sooner the better."

I blinked in surprise. Yeah. Okay. So, not a compliment.

Conner continued staring at the cat. "But everyone who meets you falls in love with you. I don't get it." His voice softened. "But I do see that I had better give you a real chance."

My face burned. "Why did you agree to come if you had no intention of treating me nicely?"

He jerked his head up, his eyes wide. Color crept into his face. After a moment, his shoulders slumped. "I was being a jerk wasn't I?"

I nodded. "I understand that we don't know each other well, but that's what we're supposed to be doing on this *outing*."

He winced.

I sighed. "And I know it's my fault that things started off so poorly. I promise, I never meant to ruin things between us before they actually started."

"I thought maybe … maybe we were doomed from the start. I guess, I wasn't trying to fix it either."

"Do you still want to give us a try?" I held his gaze. "And not just because your cat likes me but … because you do?"

He lifted one side of his mouth into a smile. "I do … like you." He snorted. "I liked you before Henry here did, although he seems to be doing a better job showing it."

I smiled and nuzzled the cat again, then met Conner's eyes. "Shall we start over?"

He nodded.

I held out my hand. "I'm Michelle Watson. I have an identical twin, two older brothers, and my parents live in Chattanooga; and although it's been months since I broke up with my boyfriend, we're still best friends and, believe it or not, this is the first date I've had since we broke up."

Conner winced. "Really?"

"Yeah," I whispered, emotion rising to the surface again. Sometimes being emotional wasn't in my favor. I couldn't control the random times something would prick me.

He reached out and ran a hand across the cat's back.

Henry flicked him a look but allowed it.

"How long were you together?"

"About a year and a half."

He whistled low. "That's … tough."

"Yeah," I whispered. "It is. We're just now starting to explore other options." I saw Kyle's pained expression at my door in my mind's eye and tried not to focus on it. "I … never got around to telling him that you and I had made plans. I didn't know he was coming over, and …" I wrinkled my nose. "It was awkward … for all of us."

His soft eyes shone with compassion. "I'm sorry. I keep jumping to conclusions with you. But … I had a girlfriend cheat on me and well …"

"Yikes."

"Yeah."

I put the cat down. Rising to my full height, I dusted cat hair off of my shirt. "Well, how about this date? It is a date now, isn't it? Not an outing?"

Conner's cheeks pinked again. "It's a date. And I'm really sorry for my behavior. I can't seem to get it right with you, and I really want to."

"Forgiven." I stepped toward him, then stopped. "Oh, there is one other thing." I hesitated. "The overpriced coffee."

He held up a hand. "Sorry. I was just being cranky. I can't fathom why anyone would waste the money, but it's not my place to say."

I laid a hand on his arm. "I … co-own the shop."

He closed his eyes and groaned. "And I put my foot in my mouth. Again. I am so sorry."

I squeezed his arm. "It's okay. Honest. After everything I did … I just want to put it all behind us."

He gave me an uncertain smile. "Is it at least good coffee?"

I grinned. "The best in town."

His smile slowly widened as we stared at each other. "You're very pretty," he whispered, probably without meaning to because his face darkened again as soon as the words were out of his mouth.

I giggled. "People say I look just like my sister, but I don't see it."

He laughed, looking more relaxed.

"So where are we going?"

"Are you sure you still want to? I wouldn't blame you if you wanted to go home."

I slid my hand into his. "I really do. I've been looking forward to our date."

His grip tightened. "Okay. I thought we'd ride out to the creek. There's a pretty spot. We can take the horses or the tractor. Your call."

I wrinkled my nose. "Let's go with the tractor today."

"You've never ridden a horse?"

I shook my head.

"Wouldn't you want to?"

"I don't know. It sounds like a good way to fall and break my neck."

"I wouldn't let you fall." His eyes softened. "Maybe next time?"

A warmth tingled out from my chest. "Next time sounds great."

―――――――――

Four weeks later ...

I sank onto the couch, pulled my feet up, and stared at my phone screen.

Conner hadn't texted which meant we were still on for tonight.

My stomach tightened with guilt and regret. I wanted him to text. I wanted him to cancel our plans. And I hated how badly I secretly begged for him to do exactly that.

Chelsea slipped in and took the other end of the couch. "Going out with Conner tonight?"

"Maybe."

She froze and eyed me, brow hiked. "Maybe?"

"If ... neither of us cancels first."

"Why would you cancel?"

I shrugged.

She sighed. "You're going to dump him, aren't you?"

"Maybe. Maybe … not."

"What's wrong with him?"

"Nothing."

She groaned. "Are you looking for a fixer-upper or something?"

I snorted. "No … I'm looking for … chemistry," I said with a great exhale. There was a lightness in my soul. Chemistry. I grinned to myself. That's what we were missing. Chemistry.

Chelsea must have heard me loud and clear because she groaned louder. "I thought you said that you had chemistry?"

"We did. *Did*. We don't anymore."

She squeezed her eyes closed, but I knew they were rolled in the back of her head as far as she could manage to send them. "He's a great guy. What more could you possibly need?"

"Chemistry. I already told you."

"Shells."

"Sea."

We glared at one another.

"You had chemistry with Kyle, right?"

"Yes."

"And you broke up with him?"

"Yes."

"You had chemistry with Conner?"

"Yes."

"And you're ready to break up with him?"

"Yes."

"Do you not see the pattern here?"

My chest tightened, and I strained for breath. I shook my head. "Something's not right, Sea."

"Then why haven't you broken it off with him already?"

94

"I needed to make sure."

"And you're sure now? This isn't some emotional decision, is it?"

My mind raced. Was I sure? Other than the rough start of our first date, we got along great. But the more we got to know each other, the more distant we became somehow.

"Shells?"

The tone of her voice sent my hair standing on end. "Yeah?"

"Are you still in love with Kyle?"

"No." My answer came out smooth and easy. Nothing could have been weirder than that first week Conner and I dated, but Kyle was talking to Alisson a great deal more now, and we were finding a new footing as friends.

"Are you sure?"

I did pause then, picturing Kyle's warm gaze. My heart turned over. Kyle was … I opened my mouth to answer, but nothing came out. I met Chelsea's eyes. "Do you know what I *do* know?"

"What?"

"I'm not falling in love with Conner."

She frowned.

I lifted a helpless shoulder. "I can't help it, Sea. I want a guy who excites me. I don't want to ever outgrow that feeling."

"I think you're chasing rainbows."

I stared out over her shoulder at the wall behind her. "Maybe I am." I met her concerned eyes again. "But I'm not ready to stop. I'm not ready to be with Kyle for the rest of my life." My throat tightened around my sudden confession.

She sent me a pained look.

I fought to clear my watery eyes. "I can't, Sea … I just can't. I love him, but … I can't. And Conner …" I cleared my throat. "I don't want to hurt him. But I can't ignore it anymore. All week I kept wishing he'd cancel on me. That's not normal."

"Then why haven't you broken up with him already?"

Tears burned in my eyes. "I don't want to."

"Shells. Make up your mind."

"No. I ... What if there's something wrong with me, Sea? What if I can't – won't – stay attached to anyone? I just ... really want him to make this call."

Her expression softened. She reached for my hand. "Maybe ... you're already attached to someone but aren't ready for marriage, like you said."

I bit my lip. Maybe. Maybe not. Why were feelings so hard to navigate?

"They wouldn't be if you didn't make every decision based on them," Chelsea answered my unvoiced question.

"Why do you think I hesitated all week, praying he'd be the one to break it off with me?"

She sent me a look. "Praying?"

I pouted. "Yes, praying."

She tugged on my hand. "If you were praying for him to break up with you, then you most certainly need to break up with him. You won't feel any better dragging this out. And it's clear your mind is already made up."

The thought of pulling the plug once and for all brought a bolt of light with it. Like glimpsing freedom on the other end of the tunnel.

I shot off the couch. "I'm doing it."

Chelsea blinked. "Are you sure?"

"Yes. You're right. I keep questioning whether it's right or wrong, but I've known the answer this entire time. It's not changing, no matter how many times I've asked myself. I just need to accept facts and move on."

New life coursed through my body. "You know what I want to do tonight?" Freedom. Sweet freedom. I wasn't going on a date tonight, so I was suddenly free to do anything and everything. Not waiting for her to answer, I said, "I'm going to go pick up some iced coffees. It feels like a puzzle and mystery night tonight."

She smirked. "You'd rather stay home than go out on a date? Yep, you must be ready to call it quits."

I winked. I knew my mind now, and I was about to be free. Before I could talk myself out of it, I called Conner and strode out of the room.

"Michelle? What's up?"

"Hey, Conner. I ... uhh ... well, it's about tonight." Now that I had him on the line, I was about to hurl.

He grew quiet. "You thinking about canceling?"

"Yeah."

He exhaled. "That's good. I ... uhh ... had been considering it myself."

"Really?" I said, my voice far brighter than it should have been for a breakup.

Conner chuckled. "Yeah. That's terrible, I know, but ... You're great and all, but I just don't ..."

"We're not clicking right."

"No. No, we're not."

"I feel the same way. Which stinks because you are a great guy."

"Exactly ... about you," he said with a laugh.

"So ... friends?"

"Friends. And, hey, I'll even stop by and overpay for my coffee from time to time."

I laughed. "Just bring us some watermelon, and we'll call it even."

"Alright. Deal."

We hung up and after sharing the details with Chelsea, I left for the coffee shop. The rich aroma of a good brew hung in the air. I breathed deeply as I closed the door behind me.

Harv was here but not behind the counter.

A customer, a man in a crisp dark gray suit, stood alone at the counter, staring at the menu.

I peeked over his shoulder. "Do you need some help deciding?"

He jerked to attention and looked at me, blinking as if he just woke up. "N-no. I'm just getting a black coffee."

I stared in disbelief. "You have to study the menu that long to decide on a plain-Jane coffee?"

His brows lowered. "Nooo. I was just waiting to order."

It was my turn to jerk back in surprise. "Waiting to order?" I scanned the work area, but all was still and quiet. I angled to peer around the man at the counter. The bell was missing. Great. With a huff, I strode behind the counter. "Harv!"

I pulled the bell out and laid it on the counter. I slapped my hand over it repeatedly. Turning around, I started the espressos for two iced coffees. Then reached for a large cup and the coffee pot.

Harv shot out of the office, then sighed when he saw me. "Oh, it's just you."

"Just me?" I pointed a thumb at the customer. "I'm not alone." He eyed the customer, his brows lowering in confusion.

"No, no," I said with a wiggle of my finger. I held the uncapped coffee in my other hand. "He's not my date. By the way … I'm not dating anyone." The smell of the stranger's coffee wafted up to my nose. I sniffed it, shook my head, then poured it out. I started a new pot.

Harv's mouth fell open. "But I thought you had a date tonight?"

"I did. Don't anymore."

I pumped in salted caramel for Chelsea and vanilla for myself into two empty cups and waited for the espressos to finish.

"What happened?"

I waved off Harv's concern, then cast the customer a long look. "You look like a blueberry guy. Do you like blueberries?"

He shrugged. "They're alright."

I nodded and reached into the muffin cabinet, bagging two blueberry muffins for the stranger for his wait and a couple for me and Chelsea to snack on. "The breakup was mutual. We just weren't clicking. How has your day gone?"

Harv related what little news he had while I finished off our coffees and poured the stranger's. I slid the coffee and muffins to him, smiling from ear to ear.

"What do I owe you?"

I lifted a shoulder. "It's on the house."

"Michelle," Harv hissed.

The stranger looked from me to Harv. "No, really." He reached for his wallet.

I held up a hand. To Harv, I said, "You made him wait."

Harv's mouth fell open. "I was … working on the …" He pointed to the office.

I shrugged. "You should have pulled the bell out."

He huffed and put his hands up, giving up already. "I need to get back to the computer. Is the bell out now?"

"Sure is." I kissed his cheek. "Enjoy your night."

He softened and nodded, then headed to the office.

I turned back to the customer, who was still standing there. With a tilt of my head, I asked, "Did you need something else?"

"I don't want to get you in trouble with your boss."

"I'm the co-owner." I winked. "He's stuck with me."

He cracked a smile. A very handsome smile.

Something warm lit in my chest.

Stuffing the iced coffees in a cup holder, I strode out from behind the counter.

The stranger looked back, holding the door with his body so I could pass before him.

I peered up at him with a smile as I walked through. "Thank you."

"You're welcome." His deep voice wrapped around me, tempting me to snuggle in, but I didn't.

I did, however, turn back. "You'll be back soon?"

He shrugged. "If the coffee is any good."

I couldn't contain my smile. "Then I'll see you real soon."

"You sound confident in your coffee."

"Oh, I am. But it's the muffins that will seal the deal. It's my personal recipe, and I'm very proud of them."

He nodded, his face blank, but his eyes held a touch of merriment. "I'll be the judge of that."

I smirked. "Fair enough."

We both walked around the corner of the building where our cars were parked side by side.

I placed my stuff inside, then stopped before getting in my seat. "Sorry for the wait. Our service usually is much better."

He opened his door. "Don't worry about it. I don't mind waiting." He lifted his drink. "But thank you."

I held his gaze a moment longer. There was nothing more for either of us to say, but I wanted to linger with him anyway. I smiled to myself. Breaking it off with Conner was the right move. I wasn't finished chasing rainbows.

I got in the car. I didn't know what the Lord had in store for me and my future, but I looked forward to figuring that out together.

AUTHOR'S NOTE

We did it. We wrote a story in a month ... and our newsletter subscribers got to be an active part!

Chaos we Unravel started out innocently enough. Amanda asked Anita if she had any ideas for a special July 4th newsletter. One hour later, we both decided to write a story and send installments each week for the whole month of July (for the record, Amanda is Chelsea ... so if you can imagine how Chelsea would do with that plan, you know how Amanda felt about it!).

But it was a blast! We sent two chapters to our newsletter subscribers each week and they emailed us with their suspicions and questions—and, in some ways, helped shape the story. In fact, Conner's entire character was created by our readers. Months earlier, one of our readers had suggested that Michelle date a farmer. Amanda groaned at the idea of adding to Michelle's already complicated love life, but Anita was thrilled with the idea, and Conner was born. He was never intended to be a suspect. The idea was for him to be a bit shy and awkward around Michelle, but his struggles around women made him look suspicious. Since we were listening to our readers' suspicions after each chapter, we decided to play into their idea and Conner was elevated to a real suspect.

We loved capturing the cozy town of Maple Springs during a family holiday event and hope you did too.

A special thank you to Kim Hampton for her help with editing the final copy. And Rachel Tero for her iced coffee knowledge!

If you love Maple Springs and don't want to miss any of Chelsea and Michelle's adventures (or random times we decide to write a story in a month and send it out), subscribe to our newsletter.

Your cozy mystery sisters,
Chelsea Michelle
(Amanda Tero and A.M. Heath)

CONNECT WITH US ONLINE

Join our newsletter to stay updated with new Chelsea Michelle mysteries
  chelsea-michelle.ck.page
  or scan QR code

Follow our YouTube channel because we're fun! ;) You'll also get the super inside scoop.
  youtube.com/@chelseamichelle
  or scan QR code

Join our Facebook Group to help us brainstorm and stay in touch
  facebook.com/groups/chelseamichelle
  or scan QR code

TELL US YOUR SUSPICIONS

The fun doesn't stop here!

We know the best part about sharing a good mystery is being able to share your sleuthing skills. So we've created a way for you to do exactly that.

Fill out our Did You Solve It poll, then be on the lookout for the results. We'll let you know if your gut instincts were in the majority or the minority.

Fill out the poll: forms.gle/UamattE3H1eshuS26

A serial killer. A dangerous road. And a cell phone going straight to voicemail…

A string of murders happening just across the state line makes residents of idyllic Maple Springs nervous. While Michelle Watson is obsessed with finding the killer's pattern, her twin Chelsea disagrees with her involvement.

Reading the victims' stories makes Michelle face the decisions she's been trying to ignore. Determined to live her life to the fullest, she makes an innocent choice that takes a life-threatening turn.

When Michelle stops answering her phone, Chelsea can't ignore the feeling that something is wrong. Very wrong. With friends and family, Chelsea sets out to find her sister, all while questioning if her faith is strong enough to weather the trial.

Time is running out and the last thing Chelsea wants to do is file a missing person's report for her twin.

Mini Mystery #1

Get here:

Amazon

A shocking fire. A hidden murder. And an innocent man accused.

When a devastating house fire claims the life of local contractor Morris Cummings, the community immediately starts gossiping. While no one got along with Morris, the immediate suspect is Michelle Watson's business partner—a kind-hearted elderly man who also happens to be Morris's brother. Despite his gentle nature, the mounting evidence points squarely at Harv.

Unwilling to let an innocent man take the fall, Michelle investigates behind her police ex-boyfriend's back. She enlists the help of her reluctant twin sister, Chelsea, whose position at Maple Springs Community Bank gives her important access to money trails.

As they track down leads and interview suspects, loyalties are overturned and faith is tested in a way that Chelsea and Michelle have never faced before.

Mystery #1

ABOUT CHELSEA MICHELLE

Christian authors, Amanda Tero and A.M. Heath bring you faith-based, cozy mysteries under Chelsea Michelle.

Anita, Amanda

Amanda Tero grew up attending a one room school with her eleven siblings—and loved it! She also fell in love with reading to the point her mom withheld her books to get her to do her chores. That love of reading turned into a love of writing YA fiction. Amanda is a music teacher by day and a literary guide by night, creating stories that whisk readers off to new eras and introduce them to heroic but flawed characters that live out their faith in astonishing ways.

Visit Amanda Tero at amandatero.com

A.M. Heath is the author of the 2022 Selah Finalist, Painted Memories. She enjoys writing stories that entertain while feeding the soul in contemporary and historical settings.

When away from her desk, she's a faithful member of her local church where she teaches a ladies' Sunday School class. She is happily married and raising four kids while embracing the small-town lifestyle and tightly woven family bonds.

Visit A.M. Heath at christianauthoramheath.net

BEFORE CHELSEA MICHELLE

LIBRARIANS OF
WILLOW HOLLOW

FOUR PACKHORSE LIBRARIANS FIND
ADVENTURES OUTSIDE THE BOOKS THEY CARRY.

amandatero.com | faithblum.com | christianauthoramheath.net | aliciagruggieri.com

Long before Chelsea Michelle became reality, Amanda and Anita joined two other authors in the collection, *Librarians of Willow Hollow*. If you love historical fiction with strong faith themes, this series is for you!

A Strand of Hope by Amanda Tero

Lena Davis is the daughter her mom never wanted.

But she survived. Through stories. Because books didn't judge. Books weren't angry she was alive. Books never expected her to be anything but who she was.

As she grows up, her beloved library becomes her true home. So when the library is designated part of President Roosevelt's

Packhorse Library Project, Lena is determined to get the job of bringing books to highlanders, believing she'll finally be free of her mom forever.

But earning the trust of highlanders is harder than she imagined, and her passion for books might not be enough to free her from her chains.

I Love to Tell the Story by Faith Blum

Her heart is in the right place...

Bored with her life in Castle Town, Montana, Lillian Sullivan follows her friend's suggestion and joins the horseback librarian program in rural Kentucky. Not only does she anticipate sharing her love of books, but she also wants to spread the gospel among the mountain people.

However, Willow Hollow presents her with one trouble after another and she struggles to step outside her shyness to share the gospel.

What will it take for Lillian to share her love of the Best Story? Can the power of the gospel overcome the shyness of her own heart?

Hearts on Lonely Mountain by A.M. Heath

Can two lonely people find more than a fleeting friendship or will a prejudiced town keep them apart?

When Ivory Bledsoe left the city to minister to the people of the rural mountain town of Willow Hollow, she never expected to be shunned rather than welcomed. Seeing the town as a lost cause, she's eager to return home, but when the bridge leading out of town is washed away during a flood, she finds herself stranded in the last place she wants to be.

Ben Thrasher was content with his quiet life until he met the new librarian. He can't help but be drawn to the friendly and lively Ivory Bledsoe, despite her being at the center of the town's latest superstition. It's only a matter of time until she captures his heart, turning his world upside down in the process.

Has Ivory gotten God's plan for her all wrong or is there still a way she can serve these people? And can Ben ask her to stay in a place where so few are willing to embrace her?

The Secret Place of Thunder by Alicia G. Ruggieri

Edna Sue O'Connell came back to the Kentucky hills out of duty and can't wait for the chance to escape again. Her work as a horseback librarian in rural Appalachia provides enough income for her invalid father to survive in the midst of the Great Depression, but it affords her with little else.

When an opportunity arises for Edna to take on an additional book delivery area, she spies a glimmer of hope that she might find a way out of Willow Hollow after all… and that she might actually make something of her life apart from the tragedy that has filled it thus far.

But the new routes give Edna more than she ever bargained for. Slowly, she finds that the mountains contain many valuable secrets – if she has the grit to meet them.

The Librarian of Willow Hollow series is available in paperback and eBook on Amazon.

MORE FROM AMANDA

Amanda Tero went straight from phonetics to scribbling before she understood spelling. Though none of her one-inch letters will ever be published, she has since grown up and introduced the world to her faith-filled novellas: A Strand of Hope (#1 new release on Amazon), Journey to Love, and the Tales of Faith series.

She's a picky bibliophile on a quest to fill bookshelves with pages of clean, accurate, and edifying stories, specifically for the YA Christian reader.

Her childhood as one of twelve kids in a preacher's home gave her many lessons on Biblical forgiveness, endurance, friendship, and love. She weaves this knowledge into the lives of characters who take the daring, difficult, and daunting paths, leaving readers with a glimpse of how to apply Scriptural teachings in realistic ways.

When she's not surrounded by words, Amanda educates students in understanding a different alphabet on piano and violin.

Connect with Amanda:
Email: amanda@amandatero.com
Website: amandatero.com
Amazon: amazon.com/author/amandatero
Facebook: facebook.com/amandateroauthor
Instagram: instagram.com/amandateroauthor
Goodreads: goodreads.com/AmandaTero
BookBub: bookbub.com/profile/amanda-tero

Befriending the Beast

Belle has returned unannounced to the castle to restore her relationship with the king, her father. Her hopes are dashed with the devastating message: "The king refuses to see you." Convinced that God has led her home, she is unwilling to return to Lord and Lady Kiralyn.

Time is running out for the decision that will change her life. When tragedy strikes, will she and her father be pulled further apart or knit together? Could she stay at the castle even if she will never see her father again?

The Secret Slipper

Being a cripple is only the beginning of Lia's troubles. It seems as if Bioti's goal in life is to make Lia as miserable as possible. If Lia's purpose is to be a slave, then why did God make her a cripple? How can He make something beautiful out of her deformity?

Raoul never questioned the death of his daughter until someone reports her whereabouts. If Ellia is still alive, how has she survived these ten years with her deformity? When Raoul doesn't know who to trust, can he trust God to keep Ellia safe when evidence reveals Bioti's dangerous character?

As time brings more hindrances, will Raoul find Ellia, or will she forever be lost to the father she doesn't even know is searching for her?

Protecting the Poor

Sheriff Feroci is now lord over the province, and Abtshire has become a pit of injustice. Being forced into the lord's service does not give Dumphey as many opportunities to help the poor as he desires. When attempts on his life drive him into the forest, this freedom opens a world of possibilities for helping others. But how can he do so when he is running for his life? And does God want him to do more than simply feed the poor?

Noel has always hidden behind the shadow of his older brother, Dumphey. When life forces him to stand on his own, will he still follow God in the corrupt world in which he lives? Would God really call him to do something that is beyond his power to do?

As Lord Feroci's sinister plot comes to light, each lad has a choice to make. A choice that could cost them their lives.

MORE FROM A.M. HEATH

A.M. Heath is the author of the 2022 Selah Finalist, Painted Memories. She enjoys writing stories that entertain while feeding the soul in contemporary and historical settings. Under the pen name Chelsea Michelle, she co-authors Christian cozy mysteries.

She's passionate about cheering on fellow Christian authors. She has founded the yearly writing event Author Olympics and runs the Facebook group Christian Fiction Writers' Clinic.

When away from her desk, she's a faithful member of her local church where she teaches a ladies' Sunday School class. She is happily married and raising four kids while embracing the small-town lifestyle and southern standard of back porch relaxing, sweet tea, homemade comfort food, strong Christian values, and tightly woven family bonds.

Connect with A.M. Heath:
Newsletter: eepurl.com/dDbVNz
Website: christianauthoramheath.net
Blog: christianauthoramheath.net/blog
Facebook: facebook.com/AMHeathfanpage
Goodreads: goodreads.com/author/show/8302606.A_M_Heath
Pinterest: pinterest.com/aheath2257/?eq=a.m.&etslf=5672
BookBub: bookbub.com/profile/a-m-heath
Instagram: instagram.com/fictionauthor.amheath/

Snuggle up with this growing series of Christmas romances full of hope, laughter, family, and all the traditions of the season!

Project Scrooge:

Can Scrooge find love from a friendship gone cold?

Sanford Stone cut ties with his best friend, Natalie, in favor of the love of his life ... a woman who ended up walking out on him just before Christmas. Six years later, Sanford can't bring himself to celebrate Christ's birth with any joy. Little does he know, his grandmother and her companions have dubbed him the Scrooge and intend to help him overcome his bitterness and find happiness again.

The only thing that has hurt Natalie Dunivan more than Sanford cutting her out of his life has been watching his long-held grudges slowly destroy the man she has always loved. Together with Ms. Carol, Natalie devises a plan to reach out to Sanford.

Sanford accepts his grandmother's challenge to celebrate Christmas for 31 straight days, but he didn't count on her plan involving Natalie. Can his family and friends help their Scrooge see the error of his ways, or will Natalie's presence only make things worse?

The Engagement Cover:

He nearly ruined her life. Now he's the only one who can help her.

After a disastrous dating app experience that nearly destroyed her modeling career, Teresa Bradford knows what she wants, and Justin Reynolds seems to check every box. But when her family pressures her to bring him home as her fiancé in order to ease the mind of her dying grandmother, their relationship takes a weird turn, and his absences create the need for a fill-in fiancé.

Since his mom's passing, and with his dad working out of state through the holidays, Alex Landry misses the feeling of home. So, when his friend Marc Bradford asks him for a strange favor with the promise of family for the holidays and all the tamales he can eat, he's all in. What he didn't expect was Marc's sister to be the girl he'd gone on an awful date with two years ago.

Committed to a fake engagement to fulfill a dying woman's wish, Alex and Teresa form a rocky friendship. As first impressions change and it becomes clear that Alex fits in better with her family than Justin does, Teresa is forced to reconsider what she wants. She's drawn to both men for different reasons, but the one who nearly ruined her life might be the one to help her find what truly matters.

It Came Upon a Midnight Clear:

Can a cozy inn at Christmas transform the troubled hearts seeking refuge there?

Pregnant and alone, Alissa Hill moved to Garland, Tennessee to help at her aunt's inn. When a guest brings her hidden past to the inn's door, she must decide whether to face it or continue to run.

A career-ending injury ruined Stephen Powell's life plans. Now a former NFL kicker, he's searching for a new purpose while recovering at the Cheery Inn. But those at the inn may offer him much more than he expects.

Sparks fly the moment Alissa and Stephen meet, but secrets and regrets may keep them apart unless they can learn to forgive and move beyond their brokenness.

Read this heartwarming Christmas romance today!

www.ingramcontent.com/pod-product-compliance
Lightning Source LLC
Chambersburg PA
CBHW070604180626
46817CB00005B/1987

* 9 781942 931355 *